"I'm no more a gentleman than you are a lady."

Matthew's voice was rough around the edges.

"But I am a lady!" Charity cried. "That's exactly what I've been trying to tell you."

"There are some things you tell, and some things you show." There was a glittering blue mystery in his eyes, and his voice was lethally soft, like a snake rustling through dry grass. "Your eyes are inviting me."

"Your audacity is unbelievable!" she protested, but without half the conviction she would have liked.

"Let's quit talking and just find out," he suggested lazily. "Is she a lady or isn't she?"

She saw him leaning alarmingly closer. She saw it and had plenty of time to run. To move away from him. To turn her head. To be a lady....

But she didn't.

Quinn Wilder, a Canadian writer, was born and raised in Calgary, but now lives in British Columbia's Okanagan Valley, away from the bustle of a city. She has had a variety of jobs, but this journalism graduate's favorite pastime has always been writing. As a freelancer, Quinn's list of credits includes magazine articles, educational material, scripts and speeches. Her first novel became a Harlequin Romance—a high point in her career. She enjoys camping, skiing and horseback riding.

Books by Quinn Wilder

HARLEQUIN ROMANCE

2772—THAT MAN FROM TEXAS
2886—TO TAME A WILD HEART
2904—DAUGHTER OF THE STARS
3096—HIGH HEAVEN
3191—OUTLAW HEART
3258—RIDE A STORM
3273—DEVON'S DESIRE

ONE SHINING SUMMER

Quinn Wilder

Harlequin Books

TORONTO • NEW YORK • LONDON
AMSTERDAM • PARIS • SYDNEY • HAMBURG
STOCKHOLM • ATHENS • TOKYO • MILAN
MADRID • WARSAW • BUDAPEST • AUCKLAND

ISBN 0-373-03314-1

ONE SHINING SUMMER

This edition published by arrangement with Harlequin Enterprises B. V.

Printed in U.S.A.

CHAPTER ONE

"THERE HE IS! The mystery man!"

"Gee," Charity Marlowe responded dryly from where she sat in a decrepit upholstered chair, her head thrown back, her hair hidden under a towel, and her eyes clenched tightly shut. "He's just a few minutes early for the unveiling of the new me. Could you ask him to come back later?"

There was no answer to her gibe, and, despite the fact that the fumes in the room told her the substance on her hair was likely to blind her if it made contact, she sat up and risked opening one eye.

She could see the entire cabin in one quick—very quick—glance, and her cousin had disappeared.

"Mandy," she cried, "come back here. You know the instructions said not to leave this stuff too long..."

"Mmm. I'll be right there, Char," Mandy's voice drifted in the open door.

The minutes dragged by. Charity noticed it was already hot in the cabin. If it was like this at the end of May, it was going to be insufferable by July and August.

"I'm crazy," she muttered to herself, and then smiled. It felt good to be just a little bit crazy for once in her life. "Mandy!" she called again.

This time there was no response and, sighing, she pulled the towel more tightly around her head, got up out of the chair and went to the door. Her throat closed with pleasure as she looked out. The cabins were located high on the side of a steep hill.

"Only staff could be asked to climb a set of stairs like this," Mandy had panted as they had wrestled Charity's suitcases up the hill yesterday.

But because of the height they looked right over the roof of the main building of Anpetuwi Lodge. From where she stood, Charity could see the tranquil green-watered cove, and the darker, sparkling blue waters of the Okanagan Lake beyond. The freshness of the air nearly took her breath away, the air ripe with the woodsy smells of cedar and pine, sunshine touching earth.

She wrapped her arms around herself and sighed. Not so crazy after all.

And then she noticed what her cousin was doing.

"Mandy!"

"I've colored hair lots of times," Mandy muttered, not removing her eyes from the binoculars she had screwed into them. "Quit worrying."

"I'm not worried about my hair." That was only partly true. "I don't think it's ethical for you to be spying on the lodge's guests."

"Come on, Doc." Mandy managed to pull herself away from the glasses long enough to roll green eyes at her cousin and wrinkle her freckled nose. "What's unethical about admiring a good-looking man?"

"Through *binoculars*," Charity reminded her, but she was smiling. How could one not smile around someone as irrepressible as her gorgeous red-headed cousin?

"A technicality," Mandy said with a sniff, and returned the binoculars to the main lodge.

"Mandy, maybe you shouldn't call me Doc, even jokingly. It might—"

"Oh, right! Blow your cover!"

"Well, it was you who said that—"

"Darn right! People are absolutely not going to like ordering their beer from a doctor. My slip. It won't happen again. Besides—" again she pried her eyes away from the eyeglasses and looked at her cousin "—in just a few minutes you are going to be transformed into a *femme fatale*. No one would ever guess that the studious, nondescript—"

"I get the idea," Charity said wryly. "Speaking of which, don't you think we'd better get this glop off my hair before it turns it green?"

"I told you, I've done streaking before. You can leave that stuff on practically forever without it doing any harm." Mandy's tone implied that green might be an improvement over Charity's natural color—an admittedly mousy shade of brown.

Mandy was peering through the binoculars with the intensity of an army scout who had just discovered the enemy, and with a defeated sigh Charity let her own gaze drift in the same direction.

The unsuspecting object of Mandy's interest had come out of his room in the main lodge and was on what he probably assumed was an immensely private balcony. He was reading a newspaper. Not dreadfully exciting stuff, and yet Charity could reluctantly understand why her cousin found the man intriguing and was having trouble looking away. There was something arresting about him, a masculine potency that leapt the physical chasm that separated them from him with alarming ease.

Strength. His strength was evident even in the distance. She could easily see the broadness of his shoulders underneath a tailored white sports shirt. Long, muscled legs were shown to full advantage by a pair of crisp khaki shorts. He was tanned, and had curly dark hair that glinted in the late-afternoon sunshine. Though too far away to see his facial features clearly, Charity had an impression, again, of strength. Cool, composed strength.

He shifted in his chair, the movement fluid, sending small ripples along the muscles of his legs and arms. There was an animal tension about him, something that suggested alertness, even when he was in repose.

It made Charity even more uneasy about Mandy unabashedly training the binoculars on him. Still, reluctant as she was to aid and abet her curious cousin in any way, she found herself asking with careful casualness, "What's his mystery?"

"Humph! That he's here."

"What's so mysterious about that?"

"For the whole season. The lodge doesn't even officially open until tomorrow."

"How do you know he's here for the whole summer?"

"I consider it part of my job to know everything about everybody," Mandy muttered abstractedly. "I check the bookings to get a general idea of what to plan for weekly activities. Have we got seniors or families? When are the regulars coming, and what did they like doing last year? And this guy turns up, in Room 302, week after week after week. Odd."

"I don't think it's so odd," Charity said.

Mandy sighed and pressed the field glasses at Charity. "Here. Take a look through these."

"Absolutely not!" Charity said, trying to push the glasses away.

"Well, suit yourself, but one good look and you'd know that men like that generally do not spend their summers in places like this."

"But this is a world-famous vacation retreat!" Charity protested. Somehow those confounded binoculars were up at her eyes. She fiddled with them, trying to get them to focus.

"Anpetuwi is a world-famous resort—generally favored by the geriatric set, honeymooners and young families. Single people do not flock here. Not with Club Med being in the same price range. Besides, two weeks is about as much rustic charm as most people can stand. So what's a man like that doing here? For the entire season?"

As if to help Charity answer Mandy's question, the binoculars suddenly took it upon themselves to come distinctly into focus.

The man's face was sharply and arrogantly handsome. His cheekbones were high, his nose straight as an arrow, his chin jutting, his mouth wide and sensual in spite of—or maybe because of—the stern downturn at the corner of his lips. His thick eyebrows were furrowed as he read, giving Charity an overall impression, again, of strength, but a forbidding and cold strength. Though she found it hard to judge his age, he had a look of unabashed power that only years of experience could brand on a man's face. She guessed him to be in his late thirties. Forty at the very most.

She was about to put the binoculars down ashamedly when he lifted his eyes from the paper. His eyes were a stunning dark blue, like new denim, or sapphire. And hard, too, glinting with cool lights of mockery, and sparking with something vaguely dangerous. Mandy was right. His was not the look of a man who vacationed for three and a half months in a place where bird-watching was high on the entertainment list.

"What do you think?" Mandy pressed.

Charity did guiltily drop the glasses. "A mercenary with a price on his head," she guessed, only half kidding.

"Good thought," Mandy said approvingly. "I was thinking maybe a Mafia don who'd turned State's Evidence against his Family."

"Pretty good, but he's got the most stunningly blue eyes I've ever seen."

"Does he?" Mandy said. "I always rather thought you had the market cornered on stunningly blue eyes."

"Night and day. Mine are your everyday garden-variety blue. His are dark...like where the cove water meets the lake over there."

Mandy shot her an admiring look for her observation skills. "I think Italians can have blue eyes."

"Only snapping black for Mafia dons," Charity retorted. She realized it was good to be with Mandy. Her cousin always coaxed a lighter side of her to the surface. In fact, she reminded herself, since they had been children Mandy had always had a knack for getting her somber cousin, normally something of a goody two-shoes, into a great deal of trouble.

With that in mind Charity should have firmly handed back the glasses. She should have said, I don't know where you got those things, but please put them away before somebody sees the sun glinting off them and assumes it's *me* spying on the guests.

But she didn't. Charity had been obeying her silent "shoulds" most of her life. She was one of those people who obeyed the rules, who was cautious, and *never* irresponsible. And those were qualities essential to her career in medicine—but not so essential to her carefree summer.

Feeling a fiendish sense of delight at being "bad," she lifted the binoculars back to her eyes to have one last look at the mystery guest.

She squinted through the glasses, and adjusted them slightly left. Ah, yes, there was his leg. She scanned lazily upward, appreciating the healthy lines of that extremely male body. And then . . .

Charity gave a squeak like a startled sparrow, and dropped the binoculars so swiftly that the weight jerked uncomfortably on her neck. She turned and darted into the cabin, trying to slam the door even as Mandy squeezed in behind her.

"What?"

"He was looking back!"

"He wouldn't be able to see you, silly."

"He was looking back through binoculars!"

"No!"

"I'm afraid so," Charity said dejectedly. Why was it that every single time she did one little thing that was the least bit out of line she got caught at it? Why was it that she was always with Mandy when that happened?"

"Did he look interested?" Mandy asked cheerfully.

"Interested? Mandy, I have a towel over my head. Quite frankly, he looked furious!"

"He'll probably never recognize you without the towel."

"He'll probably report me, and that will be the end of my search for a perfect summer."

"Oh, pooh. Men and women look at each other all the time."

"Through binoculars?"

"You're too serious, Char. Why imagine the worst scenario? Just think, some day you could be telling your grandchildren. 'Yes, I first saw your grandpa through a pair of binoculars. He was sitting on the balcony of Room 302 at the Anpetuwi Lodge, and he was snorting smoke.'"

"Mandy, you are hopeless." But Mandy's gift for drama and her change to a quavering old voice had brought a reluctant smile onto Charity's lips. "What am I going to say to him when I see him face-to-face? Should I apologize?"

"Of course not! I have a license to look through these," she claimed happily, tapping the binoculars. "I'll be leading the first bird-watching tour in just four days. There was a Whiskey Jack on his porch, you know. You can tell him I was pointing it out to you, should he have the bad manners to bring up the incident."

"A Whiskey what?" Charity asked, not always able to follow her cousin's wonderful leaps in logic.

"A kind of bird, not a kind of drink," Mandy said, with a giggle. "Little robbers, very common to this area, not the least bit afraid of people."

"In other words, a perfect excuse to be staring at someone's balcony. I'm ashamed of myself, Mandy, and I should hope you are, too."

"Not in the least," Mandy said.

"Mandy, I love you dearly. You are my favorite person in the whole world. You got me a summer job in heaven at a time when it felt as if my life was hell. You've talked me into contact lenses, six summer outfits and a bikini. You've changed the style and the color of my hair. But I have this niggling little doubt about whether I can get through a summer with you as my roommate and have my sanity intact."

"Humph! You'll probably learn to have fun. Wouldn't that be awful? Besides, what would your one shining summer be like without a few interesting male specimens in it?"

Charity let her eyes move to the view again. One shining summer.

Two weeks ago she had finished her internship at St. Paul's Hospital in Vancouver. Her final rotation had been on the emergency ward, and she had seen it all. Gunshot wounds. Accident victims. Beaten-up prostitutes. Drug addicts. Sometimes she had worked twenty-four hours without sleep.

She was twenty-six years old. She had looked twice that when she had limped into her cousin Mandy's apartment in Vernon, in the Okanagan Valley, burnt-out, exhausted, disillusioned and emotional. She had intended to stay for a weekend.

Mandy had plied her with tender loving care until the tears had come. The tears, and this tiny little thing within her that she hadn't even known was there.

Charity had always been smart. The family scholar. The worker. The one with the ambition and the talent and the brains to really make something of herself.

She'd started university when she was seventeen years old. Worked her way through the bachelor of science program in three years, and entered medical school on partial scholarships. She had ground her way through part-time jobs and four years of medicine and two years of internship without complaining, without ever questioning her dream to help her fellow man in the most noble way she could imagine.

And yet, sitting on Mandy's outrageously colorful couch the night of their reunion, she had realized there was a dream within her she had never acknowledged.

She wanted, just once, to be young. To have fun. To be free and spontaneous. To recapture the adventures of youth that she had missed or lost in years of stress and studying and working. Her work and studies had been so all-consuming that she had never even had a boyfriend!

She wanted, she had told Mandy dreamily, just one summer. To sit on the beach and suntan. To swim, and canoe, and walk, and sail. To listen to bird-songs, and identify foliage. To dance at night. To walk under the stars. To sit by fires and watch the moon rise. To eat hot dogs off sticks and run through sand. To listen to music and read for the pure pleasure of reading.

One summer. One shining summer so she could move into her career without feeling forever the loss of some part of herself.

Words spoken, wistfully, and then put away. But not by Mandy.

Mandy, a kindergarten teacher during the year, had worked at the famous Anpetuwi Lodge as its entertainment director for several years now during the summer. She arranged games and activities for the guests, claiming her two jobs were just about identical, except that her kindergarten children were more mature. Despite Mandy's tendency to talk about Anpetuwi as if it were an aging aunt—demanding, annoying, falling apart, and hopelessly old-fashioned—Charity knew she loved the place with her whole heart and soul. She even wondered if it might not have been Mandy's laughter-filled anecdotes about summers at the lodge that had coaxed this deep ache of loss within her to the surface of her consciousness.

Before she quite knew what hit her, Mandy had informed Charity that she had personally landed her a job as a cocktail waitress on the outdoor patio—the Susweca Lounge—at the lodge.

"How can I have a job there?" Charity had demanded. "I didn't even fill out an application form."

"Oh, things are pretty casual around the lodge," Mandy had returned. "Mrs. Foster really likes me. She's hired a number of people on my say-so."

Charity's mind, that formidable intellect that had been governing her every action for years, reminded her of the crush of student loans she had to pay. But her heart, her poor, long-neglected heart, had answered yes, before her head had even begun to calculate all the reasons she absolutely could not and should not give herself over to this madness.

She would have her summer. In the autumn she could return to Vancouver and begin substituting for doctors going on holidays or trips or to take courses until the day she had repaid her loans and could begin to look at having her own practice.

She had known as soon as they had arrived at the lodge that her heart had made the right decision, even though it felt irresponsible and utterly childish to be spending a summer like this, at her age, and after all the work she had done to put the initials M.D. after her name. Her heart had taken wing as she and Mandy had walked down into the lodge.

Motor vehicles were not allowed on the grounds. A parking lot was provided at the top of the property. A paved serpentine path wound down to the lodge through thick natural woods of cedar and pine, birch and wild cherry, oregon grape and wild huckleberry bushes.

At appointed hours, Mandy informed her, a golf cart went up and collected luggage from the covered box in the parking lot, and also delivered infirm guests up the long hill if they so requested.

It was a peaceful fifteen-minute stroll through shady woods down the hill. Birds sang riotously in the thick foliage, and squirrels squawked indignantly as they passed.

With one final corkscrew twist the path came out of the woods, flattened out and meandered along the edge of a lush expanse of green lawn. The path ended at the wide stone steps that led up to the main entrance of the lodge.

Considering the reputation of Anpetuwi, the lodge was surprisingly unpretentious. Constructed in a hexagon shape, it had been built of logs, now darkened with age. It was not particularly large or splendid, and yet it had a warmth and charm and dignity about it that appealed to Charity immediately. Once, someone had put their heart into building this place, and it was still there, somehow, in those dark, rough-hewn logs, in the French panes of glass at the windows, in the white paint of the log chinking, in the red geraniums that already bloomed, radiant, in window boxes.

To the right of the lodge were a dozen or so stone steps leading to a half-moon beach. A volleyball net was set up on it, a wharf stretched out into the cove. Upside-down canoes, red, blue, yellow and green, lay in a neat line near where the beach gave way to the majestic rocks that, except for a narrow opening, closed off the cove from the main part of Okanagan Lake.

The log staff cabins were nestled high on the hill behind the lodge. Reached by several dozen rickety wooden stairs, they were small and quaint, strung out along a boardwalk. Each had its own balcony, tiny bedroom containing two small beds and an eating-living area combined. Each also had a wood stove, and a bathroom so small that someone of Arnold Schwarzenegger proportions would have been afraid to enter it, for fear of never getting back out. Bright red gingham curtains hung cheerfully at all the windows.

Charity had felt something tug at her heart the moment she had first seen this cove. She had known with all her soul that she had made just the right decision.

It was true she didn't know anything about waiting on tables. Mandy had assured her it was a cinch, but it was the hours that had made her take the plunge into something so totally out of her realm of experience. The Susweca Lounge was open from eight at night until one in the morning. Nothing could have been more perfect for someone who *had* to work, but desperately wanted to enjoy the sunshine and activities of summer. A few hours of work at night would be a small price to pay for lolling about one of the most beautiful and secluded vacation spots in the world during the day.

Anpetuwi had been in the Foster family for generations, and Mandy had assured her that there was a complete lack of snobbery about staff mingling with guests. Mrs. Foster encouraged the staff to avail themselves of the lodge's delights. If the people who worked for her were happy, she felt, her guests were happy. Of course, her generous spirit about staff using the amenities of the lodge also allowed her to pay them a pittance that had made Charity's small salary as an intern seem princely.

"Just the summer," Charity told Mandy now, touching her cousin's arm. "Not the men."

"Humph! I'm not working on this new look so that you can spend the summer celibate, you know."

Charity shook her head. There was no sense in even trying to tell her cousin—again—that she was just not the stuff that men went wild over. She never had been. She'd always envied Mandy her wonderful looks and her voluptuous compact figure, but she had long ago accepted the fact that she and Mandy were not made of the same stuff.

"Mandy, getting my career off the ground is a challenge that is going to take a few more years of my undivided attention. This is an interlude—as uncomplicated an interlude as I can make it."

"Don't be silly. Nobody is suggesting marriage and fourteen children. But a little casual flirtation, a dollop of romance here and there, is the spice of life."

"Well, not this life," Charity said firmly. She didn't know very much about romance, to be sure, just enough to know that it seemed to be a force that did not like to be tamed and squeezed into the orderly compartments of people's lives. Romance also seemed to be diametrically opposed to peace and relaxation, which was why she had come here.

Not that she need worry, she thought ruefully. She was not exactly a romantic figure. Charity was tall, and thinner now than she had ever been, because of her last rotation with its odd hours and incredible stress. For as long as she could remember, her hair had been kept in a short no-nonsense style that wouldn't require any of her precious time to look after it. She had not had money for clothes, and neither the time nor the inclination to experiment with makeup and other items of fashion.

In short, Charity had always looked like exactly what she was—an extremely serious, clever, studious young woman. Her family had always referred to her as the "egghead."

Mandy had begun to whistle as she worked on Charity's hair.

"Can I look?" Charity demanded.

"No!"

"Why not?"

"I'm not done yet."

Mandy brought out a makeup box, and while Charity squirmed and complained she dusted on eye shadow and mascara and blusher and lipstick.

"Now can I look?" Charity demanded.

"Not just yet."

With absolutely no respect for Charity's privacy, Mandy waltzed over to her wardrobe and began rummaging around in it.

"This one," she finally decided.

Charity looked at the skirt and blouse her cousin was holding. A light blue wraparound skirt and a beautiful white silk blouse. Casual and yet somehow extraordinarily classy. And no doubt the most well-suited outfit in her wardrobe for her first meeting with her employer, Mrs. Foster, scheduled for later this afternoon.

"I can't buy this," she'd protested to her cousin just two days ago.

"You have to," Mandy had said airily. "Cocktail waitresses have to look gorgeous. Think of it as an investment that your tips will pay you back."

Charity knew she wasn't going to look gorgeous no matter what she did, and deciding she needed all the help she could get to lure in those tips that might hold off personal bankruptcy for three months, she had purchased the skirt and shirt—with six other summery, playful outfits that she would probably never be able to wear again as long as she lived.

"Can I look now?" she asked, after she had changed.

Mandy studied her critically, and then a smile tugged across her leprechaun features. "Look," she agreed.

Charity turned and looked in the faintly wavering glass behind their bedroom door.

Her mouth fell open.

A *young* woman looked back at her. A tall young woman, with hair that looked thick and wild and was streaked blond as though she had cavorted under the sun all the days of her life.

"Mandy, I think we overdid the streaking a touch," she said uncertainly.

"Nonsense. Men are crazy for blondes."

She sensed there was no use reiterating that making men "crazy" for her was not in keeping with her plans for a perfect summer.

She studied herself intently and with astonishment. Her eyes, no longer hidden behind glasses, looked large and blue as a summer sky. The way Mandy had swept her hair back from her face in such untamed curls, and the skillful dusting of makeup, accentuated the highness of her cheekbones, the delicacy of her nose, the soft fullness of her lips. For some reason the simple outfit accentuated her long legs, and made her appear willowy and lithe rather than just bony and flat-chested.

She looked as if she could be on the cover of a fashion magazine.

She turned to her cousin with tears smarting in her eyes. "What have you done to me?"

Mandy shrugged. "Given you your wish. Goodbye, Charity Marlowe, M.D. and hello, Char, sun worshiper and siren." Her tone lost its impertinence and became gentle. "I've always thought you were so pretty, and that it was such a shame to hide that behind those thick glasses, and that studious pallor. You're beautiful, Char, and it's a sin to hide that. Even doctors are allowed to be beautiful, you know."

"Doctors don't have time to be beautiful," Charity informed her ruefully. "Besides it seems . . . superficial, somehow."

"Well, you'll have all the time you need to be beautiful this summer—and that's what summer is about, for crying out loud. Being superficial. I have a lot to teach you about having fun, Char!"

"Poor you. It's a big job, but I guess somebody had to do it. But the job I'm more concerned about at this moment is being a waitress. You did leave some time in this afternoon's schedule for that little detail, didn't you?"

"One full hour," Mandy assured her. Going over to the little cupboard above an old porcelain sink, she promptly emptied it of glasses, filled each one with water and pulled a tray out from underneath the sink. "There."

"There?"

"Sure. Just walk around with that for an hour or so. By the time you don't spill it anymore, you're a waitress. Presto. A little easier than becoming a doctor, wouldn't you say?" Mandy glanced at her watch. "I'll be back in an hour to take you down for a tour of the lodge and to meet Mrs. Foster. She's a sweetie."

"Anybody who would hire a waitress without an ounce of experience must be something of a saint," Charity agreed.

"She is, but don't fall over yourself thanking her for it. In fact, I wouldn't even mention it, if I were you," Mandy advised airily. "She tends to get a bit befuddled, poor old dear."

Charity's warning lights came on. "Mandy, you did tell her I didn't have any experience, didn't you?"

"I told her everything she needed to know," Mandy said, somewhat evasively. "Well, ta ta, I'm off to see what I can discover about Mr. Mystery. I'll be back in an hour."

Charity wished the topic of Mr. Mystery had not come up again. Her heart gave a little lurch as she thought about running into him at some time, which she was bound to do. It was going to be awkward and embarrassing. She just didn't have Mandy's devil-may-care charm.

Also, looking at the loaded tray, Charity had a sinking feeling that there was slightly more to being a waitress than Mandy imagined, but the spot where Mandy had stood was empty. Resignedly she slid the tray onto her arm. It was heavier than it looked. She waddled cautiously across the living room, glaring imperiously but ineffectively at the slopping water glasses.

"Did you order the bourbon and water, sir?" she politely asked the empty high-backed chair in the living room. She took one glass off the tray, unbalanced the entire thing, and stood there looking sadly down at her water-stained skirt.

"At least I missed the blouse," she muttered to herself.

She looked at the litter of glasses around her. They were the cheap, hardy variety that didn't break easily, thankfully. Still, she'd have to clean up all the puddles of water dotted across the old linoleum floor. She had just found another large fly in the paradise of her perfect summer.

It had never occurred to her that she would not be a good waitress. She was always good at everything she did. Of course, her pursuits, even her part-time jobs, had always been somewhat more academic. She had worked in the library. She had done research for a medical writer. She had worked in a laboratory.

Never once had it occurred to her that being a waitress might be *hard*.

But not as hard as her first meeting with Mr. Mystery was going to be. What had possessed her to look through those field glasses?

CHAPTER TWO

"HIS NAME IS Matthew Blake," Mandy informed Charity as they descended the steps from their cabin onto the paved pathway that led to the lodge.

Thankfully, she hadn't even noticed that Charity had changed from the blue wraparound skirt and was now wearing red shorts with her white silk blouse. The shorts were pleated about the waist and flared widely, giving an illusion of being a too short skirt. They showed quite a lot of leg, and were undeniably sexy. They were another purchase that Charity had hesitated over, but Mandy had insisted that cocktail waitresses had to be subtly sexy at all times. She had put on a wide navy blue belt with the shorts, hoping to draw the eye away from the uncomfortable length of naked leg, but instead, because of her all too narrow waist, had managed to look even sexier than ever.

"And he's from London. Do you suppose that means London, Ontario, or London, England? I'll bet he drives that Mercedes parked up in the lot. A Mercedes! I suppose you're the only one in the Marlowe family who'll ever attain that status—"

Charity opened her mouth to say that a Mercedes was really not on her list of aspirations, but at that moment they approached a sharp twist in the path and were almost knocked over by an electric golf cart careening around it.

"Watch where you're going, Nelson!" Mandy snapped cheerfully.

Nelson, apparently unperturbed by the incident, and obviously disinclined to follow Mandy's advice, was speeding away with his head twisted over his shoulder—watching them, instead of watching the path! Two seconds before he slammed into a tree he braked to a halt, got off the cart and ambled back toward them, grinning with calculated boyish charm.

Charity was quite accustomed to her cousin's eliciting rather dramatic responses from the male population, but was a little discomfited when Nelson, a tall, rangy boy with sandy hair and nice looks, seemed to have eyes only for her.

"Hi, Mandy," he said without looking at Mandy. "Who's your friend?"

"This is my cousin, Char."

"Hi, Char," he said, straining so hard for a deep man-of-the-world note that Charity had to bite her lip to keep from laughing. "Would you care to have dinner with me tonight?"

"No, thank you," Charity said, as gently as she could. Nelson was obviously some years younger than herself, a fact that, given her new getup, was probably not at all obvious to him.

"Another time, perhaps," he said with youthful dignity, turned and galloped back to his golf cart and was up the path at full speed.

"Why didn't you say yes?" Mandy demanded as they continued along, strolling around the twist in the path and out into the open stretch of lawn.

"Yes? Oh, for heaven's sake, Mandy. He was—" she stopped. To one side of the path was a quaint wooden bench. But there was nothing quaint about the masculine form that adorned it. She felt a deep flush of embarrassment crawl up her neck as she gauged how far the sound of her and Mandy's conversation might have carried.

Please don't let him have heard what we were saying earlier, she begged inwardly. But she suspected she was out of luck. Sound carried incredibly in the bowl of landscape the lodge sat in. She could hear voices on the path behind them, and she could hear every word they were saying.

It was too awful! First, to have been caught spying on him, and then caught discussing him.

Matthew Blake was sitting, with one hand draped casually over the back of the bench, the other holding an evil-looking black cheroot. If he had looked rather large and strong from a distance, the effect was even more overpowering close up. The length of the legs protruding, muscular, tanned and hair-covered, from his shorts was now very evident. The man was at least six feet two inches. And the rock-hard cast of his muscle didn't end at his legs.

Her eyes roamed helplessly upward, noting the flatness of his stomach, the breadth of his chest and shoulders, the sinewy ripple of long arms. Finally, her eyes dared to go to his face. It was carved into planes of rugged indifference, though the blue eyes that blazed at Charity were filled with cynical censure that left her in no doubt that he had heard almost every word Mandy had uttered about him. It remained to be seen if he recognized her. She held on to the slim hope of the towel as a disguise.

"Good afternoon," she said weakly.

Mandy seemed momentarily at a loss for words. But only momentarily.

"Mr. Blake!" she said with enthusiasm, going over and plopping herself down on the bench beside him. "How nice to be able to meet you." She shoved her hand at him. Surprise tinged the dark blue of his eyes. "I'm Mandy Marlowe, the entertainment director here."

Reluctantly, Charity joined them, though she didn't sit down. For the second time in one day, she was with Mandy and the male attention was focused on *her.* It was uncomfortable, and it was particularly uncomfortable in light of the faint dislike that seemed to shade the depths of those denim dark eyes.

"And you," he directed at her, his voice deep with sarcasm, "must be Pam."

"Pam?" Charity echoed, not unaware of the faint mocking amusement that touched the corners of his stern mouth. He knew she was uncomfortable and he was enjoying it!

"If you were a man, I would have guessed Tom," he said easily, "but as it is . . ." He shrugged, his eyes never leaving her face.

She could feel the red stain crawl up her neck as she caught his drift. Peeping Tom. Or Peeping Pam, as the case might be.

The interchange had gone completely over Mandy's head. "Oh, no, this isn't Pam. This is my cousin, Char."

"I stand corrected, Misses Marlowe." He inclined his head, and the gesture should have seemed courteous, yet Charity was struck by a certain mockery in it, and in the eyes that were narrowed on her face with unrelenting and not totally flattering interest.

Childishly, she did not extend her hand. She was aware of a prickly sensation along the back of her neck warning her of danger. She was not offering her hand into the keeping of a hungry crocodile, and there was something very cold-blooded about the glitter in Mr. Blake's admittedly fascinating eyes.

"My cousin and I were just discussing you," Mandy admitted cheerfully.

Mandy's candor took him completely by surprise, and it was obvious he was not a man accustomed to being surprised. For a moment unguarded amusement tugged at the stern line of that mouth, and lit something in the haunting depth of those eyes. For a moment his attractiveness shone so powerfully that it almost sabotaged the warning bells sounding strident alarm inside Charity's head. But only for a moment.

For when he spoke his voice was cool, faintly overlaid with disapproval. "So I heard. Your cousin seems to find me very interesting."

Charity felt herself cringe with embarrassment. He obviously thought she was a man-hungry piranha, and really who could blame him? First, he'd caught himself being scrutinized through binoculars, and then heard himself being discussed with such ribald curiosity by the staff!

"Mr. Blake, I want to apologize for—"

"Being curious," Mandy cut her off blithely. "We're both incurably curious. It runs in the family." Mandy either had not noticed the formidable wall of his reserve, or had decided to batter it down with her considerable charm.

"Well, just so you can sleep tonight," he said with a certain cynical charm of his own, "it's London, England."

"Is it really?" Mandy said. Charity wondered if her cousin was capable of embarrassment. "But you're not English, are you? I don't detect an accent."

"No, I'm Canadian." He didn't elaborate, despite Mandy's turning up the full voltage of her green eyes to show that she was interested. Very interested. He was no longer looking at Mandy. His eyes had moved to Charity.

"You were saying, Miss Marlowe?"

She squirmed. He was not going to make this easy for her! "I was saying that it must have seemed a terrible invasion of your privacy to find a pair of binoculars locked on your deck earlier."

"A terrible invasion," he agreed suavely.

"I wanted to say that—"

"I was showing her a bird," Mandy interrupted, turning and wrinkling her nose in playful warning at Charity. Her expression clearly said she was being too serious.

"I'm the entertainment director," Mandy repeated, missing the undertows that were now thick in the air around her, as dark blue eyes met light blue ones and clashed like hot air hitting cold. "I hope you'll take in some of my activities."

"Bird-watching, for one?" he asked silkily.

"You know," Charity said a touch hotly, "I wasn't the only one with a pair of binoculars! What were you doing looking at the staff cabins?"

She couldn't believe she'd said that! She'd started out meaning to apologize, but there was something so darned aggravating about this man that it was turning into an accusation instead.

He smiled, revealing teeth that were straight and white. But the smile didn't make him look more attractive, it made him look more dangerous. "Perhaps I'm a bird-watcher as well."

"Humph!"

"In fact, I spotted a towel-headed man stalker. An interesting species."

So she had come across as a man-crazy huntress scouting prospects. It was so far from her real self that she might have laughed if she didn't feel so humiliated.

Mandy did laugh. "Boy, could you liven up my bird-watching expeditions! I hope you really will take in some of the activities."

"You may count on that," he said suavely, his eyes flicking briefly back to Mandy. Then that discomfiting gaze shifted once again to Charity's face. "And are you involved in entertaining the guests as well?"

His voice was a purr of pure insolence, and Charity felt shocked to the bottom of her stomach. In light of the fact that she appeared to be on the hunt, and looked like a blond bombshell, exactly what was the man asking her?

"No, I'm not," she said stiffly, as unforthcoming as he. "Mandy, we really should go," she suggested demurely.

Mandy shot her a look of pure astonishment. She had finally cornered her prey and Charity wanted to go?

But Matthew Blake did not seem prepared to let her off the hook so easily. "What job is it you have here that makes you so much more likely than the rest of your family to attain a Mercedes?" His tone was casual and conversational, even faintly teasing, but something in his eyes was coldly cutting, analyzing, weighing and measuring.

"Mandy was just teasing me," Charity said uneasily, "I'm a cocktail waitress... for the summer."

"The Mercedes is mine." His voice was a velvety caress, his eyes were still locked on hers. She could almost feel the electrical impulse of them, some challenge there that made her feel threatened . . . and yet made her heart beat a fearful tattoo inside her chest, recognizing that danger was a roller-coaster ride and that fear was often closely followed by exhilaration.

"I'm really not interested in cars," she told him flatly. Without waiting for Mandy she turned away.

"Somehow," he said softly, "a Mercedes would seem more your style than a golf cart."

She felt her shoulders stiffen. Circumstances were really conspiring against her. Even Nelson's invitation was being misconstrued as more evidence that she was some sort of siren who enjoyed luring men with her seductive powers. It was a joke, really. And certainly words would only dig her deeper in. After a few days, she was certain, everyone at the lodge would be fairly sure of who she really was. She might have to convince Mandy to adjust the wardrobe a touch, though! She turned and looked at him. Again she could see some dark and almost deadly challenge in his eyes.

"I wouldn't know," she said coolly, though her heart was making furious thunder inside her chest, "as I've never ridden in either vehicle. Mandy, I don't want to be late for our meeting with Mrs. Foster." She turned and walked away, shaking inwardly from her encounter with that bold and arrogant man.

Mandy caught up with her. "For gosh sake, Char, what's the rush?"

"That man did not like me," Charity said quietly, and added to herself, And I did not like him.

"Oh, nonsense. He practically invited you to go for a ride in his car. I think he found you intriguing! Isn't that exciting?"

Charity shivered again. "No."

"I thought he was fabulous."

"He's a good-looking man," Charity conceded woodenly.

"Sensual. Handsome. Worldly," Mandy elaborated dreamily. "And mysterious. Not too forthcoming about himself, was he?"

He'd admitted he owned the Mercedes, but it had been exactly that...an admission, rather than a revelation. It had been carefully gauged, not so much to reveal anything about himself, but rather to reveal something about them. A cat showing a mouse a bit of cheese to see what reaction he could get. But he'd made the error of showing a little too much claw at the same time.

Stubbornly, Charity resolved not to think about him any longer. She was making too much of the encounter. Hopefully her tour of the lodge would soon drive the mocking blue gaze of Matthew Blake from her mind.

It was a marvelous old building. The main door went into a small lobby with a check-in desk. Stairs on the right went up to the sixteen guest rooms. French doors led into a room that had once been the guests' lounge, but had been converted into the dining room. It still had many of the characteristics of a lounge—cluttered bookshelves took up one wall of the room. Old rifles and skis and snowshoes hung from the log walls. The tables, covered in the finest white linen and already set with bone china and heirloom silver, provided a delightful contrast.

On either side of a huge stone fireplace were more French doors. Over each one was a small wood-burned sign that announced the Susweca Lounge.

Charity went through them to her new place of employ and smiled with delight. The Susweca Lounge consisted of thirty or so small round tables on an enormous covered veranda built on stilts over the water. The view and the lake-fresh air created a wonderful atmosphere.

"It looks splendid," she said hugging herself.

"It's even prettier at night," Mandy assured her, "with the gaslights burning and the stars reflecting in the lake."

They went back through the dining room and lobby to a small office where Mrs. Foster, who was more elderly than Charity would have imagined, invited them in.

"I've lost my glasses," Mrs. Foster greeted them. "Have you seen them, Mandy, dear?"

"They're on the chain around your neck," Mandy told her gently. "Mrs. Foster, this is my cousin, Char. Remember I told you about her?"

"Did you?" Mrs. Foster asked.

"Yes. She's going to be a waitress out on the Susweca this summer."

"Ah. The Susweca. It means 'dragonfly' in Sioux, you know. Did I ever tell you that's where Paul and I met? It was a lovely night. I was sixteen and wearing my prettiest frock. All the stars were out that night. Lovely. It was lovely. Have you seen my glasses, dear?"

Mandy reached over gently and settled the glasses on her employer's nose.

"Can you tell me anything about Matthew Blake?" Mandy asked.

Charity had just succeeded in ridding her mind of that subject, and she glowered at Mandy, wondering if she ever managed to learn a lesson from anything.

"Matthew," Mrs. Foster mulled thoughtfully. "Matthew." She brightened. "Oh, yes. Matthew is such a bad-tempered boy. That's him over there." She waved in the direction of a mantel covered with obviously very old snapshots.

They listened to the old woman ramble for a bit longer then left.

"How long has she been like that?" Charity asked.

"It seems to get a little worse each year. You wouldn't have believed what a bright and with-it little woman she was when I first started here."

"How on earth does she cope with running this place?"

"Well, we all kind of do our part. Some of the staff have been here for twenty years. We all sort of know what needs to be done and do our best to do it. You know, in all the time I've worked here there has never been one single incidence of staff theft. That's usually the plague of resorts and restaurants—the staff making off with everything from sheets to T-bones. But this place is so different. It feels kind of like a family, you know? I guess we all feel intensely loyal to her."

"She should see a doctor," Charity said gently.

"We've sort of figured that—the staff—but we're scared to push it, I guess. None of us know anything about her family. They seem colossally indifferent to this place, and that makes it seem as if maybe they would be indifferent to her. We protect her as much as we can. It would just be awful if her family put her away somewhere. She's happy here, and if she's not exactly helpful anymore, at least she's harmless. We all love her pretty dearly.

"I couldn't tell if she knew Matthew Blake or not, could you?"

"I think you have Blake on the brain," Charity said in her sternest doctor's voice. "Take a complete break from your obsession and call me in two weeks."

"I suppose he might be bad-tempered—" Mandy said dubiously.

Charity snorted. Her cousin was obviously terribly afflicted. It was the most obvious thing in the world that that man had a bad temper. An evil temper, in fact.

"But no, it was probably somebody else in those pictures she was thinking of. She does have about thirty grandchildren, so I guess one of them could be a Matthew. You know, having met him, I'm no closer to guessing what he's doing here."

"Maybe he's a real-estate developer who's planning a row of condos right over there where the volleyball net is," Charity suggested uncharitably.

"You'd have to have a soul of ice!"

"Exactly," Charity muttered.

"Oh, Charity, your whole problem is that you're accustomed to people bowing down before you because you're a doctor and they assume you walk with the gods. He didn't treat you with disrespect—he just assumed you were a mere mortal like the rest of us. You look like a sexy woman and he treated you like one. You're going to have to get used to that this summer."

Charity supposed that there could be at least an element of truth in that, though she did not feel comforted. "Maybe we need to tone down the sexy image a little, Mandy. It's not me."

"Pooh," Mandy dismissed her. "I think that perhaps he's a writer. Wouldn't this be a perfect place to write a book?"

"Hmm," Charity said, unconvinced.

"What kind of books do you think he'd write?"

"Not romance," Charity said curtly.

"Adventure," Mandy decided.

"Horror," Charity corrected.

IT MIGHT NOT have been the worst night of Charity's life, but it was coming close. It was opening day for Anpetuwi and tonight the lounge was packed. Despite the fact that it was in the open air, the roof held in some of the smoke, which Charity now felt was reaching killing proportions.

She was wearing a halter dress the color of flame that had wilted in the first hour. She had people calling from all directions. She couldn't remember the names of the drinks they were ordering, and she found it nearly impossible to add up the prices of drinks for an entire table in her head.

If things weren't going badly enough, her feet hurt inside new shoes, and then *he* showed up. Thankfully, there wasn't a table to be had, but her run of luck—bad luck, that was—seemed to be holding. At precisely the minute it looked as if he might step back inside the lodge, a young couple, obviously very much in love, got up and left, leaving a place for him to sit.

By the time she got to him, he looked impatient, like a man far too accustomed to everyone in the world dropping whatever they were doing to look after his needs first.

"What can I get you, Mr. Blake?"

His eyes ran up her with casual assessment, and then stopped on her face, lazily scanning it. How dared he treat her as if it was his right to inspect her with that insolent expression on his face?

"I'll have Canadian Club and water." He leaned back and lit one of those evil-smelling cheroots.

She glared at him. She might have taken on a job as a waitress for the summer, but she was damned if she was going to let people treat her like a mindless robot because of it.

"Please," she suggested sweetly.

She had the pleasure of seeing his jaw drop. Then it snapped closed, and with his eyes narrowed he inclined his head toward her.

"I beg your pardon, Miss Marlowe. Please."

"Thank you," she said crisply. She knew she should stop there, but it was as if some little demon had seconded her tongue. "May I ask you a question?"

He shrugged, but wariness had fallen like a hood over his eyes. He took a pull on his cheroot and blew a narrow stream of pungent smoke out of those firm, sensual lips.

"Do you know what the human lungs look like?"

This was obviously not at all what he had expected. She felt smugly satisfied that she had not fed his ego by asking what he did in London, or any of the other dozen or so questions it looked as if he had been bracing himself for. He raised a surprised but mocking eyebrow. "No. Do you?"

"As a matter of fact, I do. It's an incredibly beautiful and fragile piece of your body, Mr. Blake. A healthy lung is pink and full of a honeycomb of fragile air pockets. An unhealthy lung is black and stringy. It's a good thing you don't have to wear your lungs on the outside of your chest, because it would spoil that athletic image you cultivate entirely."

She had stunned him and she knew it. She was too tired and put out to care. If she got fired, she got fired. It would be quite worth it for the expression on his face.

Then he surprised her by smiling. Ever so faintly, but it was a smile nonetheless. He crushed out the cheroot, then turned the full impact of those eyes on her.

He was puzzled, and she knew she had better be very careful about giving lectures on health to the customers. People came here to relax and enjoy themselves. This was not an office from which to be dispensing medical advice.

"Will my drink be accompanied by a lecture as well, Miss Marlowe?" His tone was dry.

She smiled faintly back at him. "Only if you drink too many of them."

She had regained her senses by the time she made her way back with his drink.

"I shouldn't have lectured you," she said, putting his drink down in front of him. "It's certainly your privilege to destroy your body if you want to."

"Somehow your apology sounds faintly like another lecture. Maybe that's a pattern. This afternoon you started out apologizing for spying on me, and ended up accusing me of spying on you."

She set down his drink so hard that it sloshed out of the glass. How could she debate that? It was true!

"You certainly seem to have an unusual interest in my body."

She could see the twinkle in his eye. She knew she was being baited, and yet she could not stop her shocked reply.

"I do not!"

He grinned. The boyish expression transformed the hard planes of his face and she stared at him as if she was seeing him for the first time. He was altogether too appealing when he did that, and he was probably well aware of it.

She collected the money for his drink, and got away from him as fast as she could.

But she couldn't really get away from him. She was aware of those sapphire-hued eyes following her from time to time, resting on her, evaluating her. Coupled with the challenges of a completely unfamiliar job, she was not sure that she had ever spent such an uncomfortable evening.

But as the evening moved on she discovered she was getting better at her job. She came up with a routine for visiting the tables, and even managed to empty a few ashtrays. Several times she felt almost caught up with the constant demands for her attention. She began to feel vaguely familiar with the names of drinks and their prices.

She avoided returning to Matthew Blake's table for as long as she could without giving him the power of knowing she was avoiding him.

"Just ice water, thanks," he said the next time she screwed up enough nerve to go back to his table. What was it about the man that set her every nerve on edge, made her tingle with an unfortunate awareness of him? And of herself, as a woman, as fragile somehow, in comparison to him?

She brought him back his drink, and then noticed with some relief that the crowd seemed to be thinning, and there was only an hour of work left.

"What does Anpetuwi mean?" he asked her, conversationally, as if he had noticed either the lull in the action, or the relaxing of some tension in her.

She stared at him. To her tired mind the question seemed unbelievably stupid. Who cared what Anpetuwi meant when she had three tables to clear, four people waving at her, and a growing list of drinks to remember when she got back to the bar?

"I have no idea, sir," she said through clenched teeth. "Would you like me to find out for you?"

"Would you?"

Go to hell. "If it means that much to you."

Mandy was sitting at a table with other staff, all of them laughing and having a wonderful time. Nelson, who was drinking rather too much, was looking at Charity more amorously by the minute.

"What does Anpetuwi mean?" she hissed at her cousin.

"Woman who lies naked on the rock," Mandy said without hesitation.

Charity eyed her suspiciously. "It does not!"

Mandy shrugged. "Have a look out there at the rock on the left of the cove opening."

Charity looked out over the balcony at the still black water toward the rocks. There was just enough moonlight to see that one of the rocks did indeed resemble a naked woman with her twin breasts thrust toward the stars.

"Oh, Lord," she muttered. She had an awful suspicion that *he* already knew exactly what Anpetuwi meant, and had asked her to embarrass her. Well, it would take a little more than that to faze someone as familiar with the human anatomy as Charity.

"And what does Susweca mean?" she asked, just for insurance. Mrs. Foster had told them what it meant yesterday, but Mandy was never much good on details and probably wouldn't recall that. If she'd lied about Anpetuwi, she'd trip herself up now.

"Dragonfly," her cousin responded.

"Great."

She didn't rush back to his table, but the next time she was passing by she stopped.

"The lodge was apparently named for the rock to the left of the cove opening," she informed him dispassionately. "Anpetuwi means woman who lies naked on the rock."

Something burned bright and hot in the bottom of those eyes. "Is that right?" he asked, one eyebrow lifted, the intense blue of those eyes asking her a different question entirely.

She gulped. "Yes, it is, and Susweca means dragonfly. It's last call. Do you want anything?"

"I guess that depends on what you're offering," he said. His voice was as sensual as raw silk, but when he saw her bewilderment his eyes drifted over to Mandy's table.

They were being watched and the whole table was in gales of laughter.

His eyes moved back to her face, a brief puzzlement darkening them. He nodded to her, got up and left.

She stared after him feeling somewhat breathless. The man certainly had impact!

She pushed him sternly from her mind. And if there was one thing Charity was good at it was disciplining her mind. She realized, wearily, almost too tired to care, that she had just been made the butt of a joke.

He had realized it before she had, and somehow the sympathy that had been briefly in those blue eyes, that she had mistaken for some sort of liking, was far more disturbing than his hard, cool look. She fervently hoped he did not drink every night.

Later, she washed down the last table and put the final glass in the dishwasher.

The bartender looked at her sympathetically. "Are you okay?"

Actually she was close to tears. Rather than having made a fortune in tips tonight, she had actually come up ten dollars short. She must have made a huge error in giving change somewhere along the line and she felt defeated.

"I'm okay," she mumbled.

"It'll come to you, Char. In two weeks everything will seem so easy to you."

No, it won't, she wanted to wail, but then she smiled at his kindness. This poor man had suffered for her inexperience all night, too. "Thank you for giving me so much help."

"That's what we're here for, love, to help one another."

She felt deeply moved that such a humanitarian statement came from such a humble source in such unexpected surroundings. Nobility could be found anywhere, and Charity allowed herself to feel faintly optimistic about her future as a cocktail waitress.

She wandered out of the lounge. It was dark and empty outside. All the customers and guests had long since departed. She felt both exhausted and keyed up, as though she would never sleep. It was a familiar feeling from her shifts on the emergency ward.

The smell of smoke clung to her clothes and skin. She felt as if she could even feel smoke, stale and greasy, in her hair.

She wandered, without really thinking, down to the side of the lake. The night was beautiful and quiet, star-studded. She clambered over some boulders, sat at the water's edge, and dribbled her aching, blistered feet through the water.

After a moment, she looked around. The night was dark and silent. She felt as if she was the only person awake in the world. The rocks she sat behind shielded her from the lodge and the staff cabins.

And suddenly she just wanted to be clean. To feel the cool freshness of the water on her heated, smoky skin, and rushing through her hair. She took off the outer layer of her clothes, hesitated for just a moment, and then peeled off her underwear. She stood and welcomed the crispness of the night air against the bare silk of her skin.

With a sigh, rather than a cry, she threw herself into the water and felt peace.

Peace that was shattered by a mocking male voice.

"So you *are* the woman who lies naked on the rock, are you?"

CHAPTER THREE

THE WATER that had seemed so bitingly refreshing only moments ago was already feeling like a straitjacket of ice tangling around Charity's speedily numbing limbs. Her teeth began to rattle as she stared at him, transfixed. Finally she forced words past shock and cold, anaethetized lips.

"Mr. Blake—"

"Given the circumstances, don't you think you are being ridiculously formal?" His voice was like the water—it gave an illusion of velvety warmth.

"Mr. Blake—" she repeated desperately, her voice trembling.

"Matthew," he insisted softly.

"Matthew," she conceded, her voice snapping with anger. But she knew he had her at a complete disadvantage, and he knew it, too. This was not the time to argue with him.

"I think you'd better get out of the water. You seem cold."

"I'm freezing, but I can't get out of the water with you there."

"Why ever not?" he asked with such assumed innocence that she felt like screaming.

"I'm not wearing a bathing suit," she snapped.

"You're not? You mean you're skinny-dipping."

"You know damn well I'm skinny-dipping."

"One of life's little pleasures," he mused. "That's why I came down here myself."

"Matthew!"

"I'll close my eyes," he said.

She regarded him suspiciously, and realized it was the best he was going to do for her.

"I'll even lend you my towel."

"That's big of you," she said curtly. He turned his back to her. A regular gentleman. She was out of the water in a split second. She found his towel, huge and fluffy, and wrapped it around herself. She was surprised that his back was still turned.

"All right," she told him.

He turned around, so that he faced the water again. He didn't even slide her a look. She watched helplessly as his hands found the buttons of his shirt. His body was washed in silver by the moonlight and when he removed his shirt she felt a tiny shiver of something that had nothing to do with the pervasive cold of the night air on her chilled skin.

He tossed the expensive silk away as though it were a rag, revealing the bold, hard contours of his chest. Dark, curling hair formed a letter T across his breast and down to his lean belly. He stood stock-still, as though he was well aware that she was totally and unwillingly mesmerized by the beauty of his physique.

And then those strong hands moved to the belt on his pants, and then the buckle, and then with tantalizing slowness to his snap and zip. The rasp of the zip going down was illogically loud in the utter silence of the night.

He stripped off his pants with unrushed ease, revealing one strong, muscled leg and then the other.

For a moment her heart caught in her throat, but then she realized he had brief, dark swimming trunks on. He moved forward, with leopardlike grace, and stood on the edge of a rock. He froze there momentarily, like a figure cast of bronze, and then stretched himself, soared upward, each of his muscles rippling, and dived. Only one small, white-highlighted ripple showed where the supple arrow of his body had pierced the water.

She located her clothes and ducked behind one of several large rocks. By just peeking over the tip of the rock she could dress and watch him, too.

He surfaced from his dive well out into the cove. His hair was slicked back, and the water ran slowly, like mercury, down the hard ridges and dips of his face. Using the rock and the darkness as cover, she watched him as he broke into motion and that powerful stroke carried him out to the rocks and back.

She had hoped she'd be long gone by the time he had finished his swim, but already he was nearly back at shore, and the filmy dress was sticking awkwardly to her still damp skin. She knew if she forced it she would rip it.

He was out of the water now, and he shook his head. The water scattered off his hair in moonlight-encrusted droplets.

With one final, desperately hard tug the dress fell into place. She stepped out from behind her rock, her skimpy dress clinging uncomfortably to her wet skin, providing absolutely no warmth, and still reeking of smoke. She wanted to turn tail and run, but she couldn't have stood herself if she appeared such a coward.

She went to him and thrust the towel at him.

"Thank you," she said. Her voice was a squeak. She didn't know why. Male bodies were certainly nothing new to her. No, that wasn't quite true. Male bodies, nearly naked, flesh rigid with cold beneath a silvery moon, were a brand-new experience to her.

Even in the half tones of night she could see the narrowing of those dangerous sapphire eyes, see sparks of desire bringing them to their full color.

"You're welcome," his lips said. But his eyes were saying something else.

Run for your life, a voice inside her head commanded her. "Good night," she said firmly, her chin tilted proudly toward the stars, as if she were royalty and not a woman sporting scraggly wet hair and a nearly see-through dress.

"Don't go." His voice was a growl.

She stood there, frozen as a statue in the moonlight, as he toweled himself off, the muscle on his arms cording and rippling and sending a faint helpless ripple through her own stomach.

He said nothing more, and his silence played across her taut nerves like a fingernail going down a blackboard. Unselfconscious of his near nakedness, he reached down to his carelessly heaped clothing and extracted his shirt from it. Finally, he turned to her, and watched her with narrow eyes. Still he was silent.

He pulled the shirt on but made no effort to button it. His broad chest heaved from the cold and his exertion. A few faint diamond droplets of water still glittered in the hair that whorled sensuously around his jewel-hard nipples.

"I should go to bed," she said weakly.

"Alone?" he asked softly.

"Mr. Blake, somehow you seem to have entirely the wrong idea about me."

"I don't know how," he said softly, but a sarcastic edge had crept into his voice. "You were watching me through binoculars. You were discussing me with your girlfriend. You were out here swimming around with not a stitch on. What kind of idea was I supposed to get?"

"You audacious, arrogant, perverted... Peeping Tom!"

"Well, if I'm a Peeping Tom that makes us about even, wouldn't you say?"

"Mr. Blake, how can I convince you I'm not the kind of woman you think I am?"

A smile curved along the sensuous line of that mouth, the most dangerous smile she had ever seen.

"Show me," he murmured. He went from frozen stillness to liquid and menacing movement in the blink of an eye.

Suddenly those flaring sapphire eyes were inches from hers, looking down at her from great heights, forcing her to lift her chin a notch higher than was comfortable to look into them. She refused to flinch, or back away, even though she was uneasily and acutely aware that his broad and mostly naked chest was a few dangerous inches from her own. She had an appalled awareness that her nipples were hard and puckered, pressed into the film of her dress.

It was probably just the sort of physiological accident that this arrogant debaucher would accept as an invitation! She folded her arms across her bosom.

"I wasn't aware there was anyone awake when I decided to swim," she informed him with regal hauteur.

"Neither was I," he snapped back.

"If you were a gentleman, you would have just backed off when you saw this place was taken!"

"I'm no gentleman," he purred.

"That is perfectly evident!" Her fickle eyes trailed down his chest. No, he was no gentleman. Chests like that belonged to a different age, a dangerous age of swashbucklers, and buccaneers who gloried in their toughness, stripped themselves to the elements, and laughed, bare-chested, into the teeth of icy sea winds.

"I'm no more a gentleman than you are a lady," he said with soft menace, his voice gone rough around the edges.

"But I am a lady!" she cried. "That's exactly what I've been trying to tell you."

"There are some things you tell, and some things you show." There was glittering blue mystery in his eyes, and his voice was lethally soft, like a snake rustling through dry grass.

"I—I don't know what you mean," she stammered.

"Your eyes are inviting me."

"They are not!" she protested, locking her wrists together when her hands seemed about to flutter up and cover those very eyes from his probing gaze.

"They're inviting me right now."

"They aren't!"

"They are. You have eyes as hot and sensuous as a blue summer sky. As sultry as a sweltering day in August. As inviting as a mountain pond faithfully reflecting the message of the sky."

"Your audacity is simply unbelievable," she spat at him, but her voice had gone faintly breathless.

"My audacity is unbelievable," he repeated softly. "Do you see what I mean about something not ringing true about you? That's not how your general run-of-the-mill cocktail waitress speaks."

"What a ridiculously patronizing statement to make," she said uneasily. "You didn't strike me as the kind of man who would put much stock in stereotypes."

"So you have given some thought to the kind of man I am, have you?" he asked with silky satisfaction.

"No!" she protested, but without half the conviction she would have liked. Her eyes had become focused on the firm line of his lips, and a scalding message raced into her belly where it clenched in a strange, anticipatory tingle.

"Let's quit talking and just find out," he suggested lazily. "Is she a lady, or isn't she?"

She saw him leaning alarmingly closer. She saw his lids droop faintly over the passionate fire that sparked the storm blue of those eyes. She saw it all, and had plenty of time to run. To move away from him. To shield her lips. To turn her head. To be a lady.

"If you kiss me," she said weakly, "I'll scream."

He smiled faintly. "No, you won't."

Again, she had plenty of opportunity to turn tail and run, to prove to him somehow, somewhere, some way, that he had got entirely the wrong idea about her.

But she stood frozen to the spot, a rabbit caught in a white light, a moth caught in its destiny with a flame.

She gasped when his lips touched her. She had expected them to be hard and hurtful, cruelly punishing. When his lips met hers, shock rippled through her because her conjectures could not have been further from the truth.

His lips touched hers like a butterfly brushing its wings against the sweet, soft petal of a flower. His lips were not steel, but silk.

Another tingling message plunged into her abdomen, where it pulsated wildly.

She didn't scream.

Tentatively, her lips returned the brush of his, and she heard a moan deep in his throat. Her stomach did an odd flip as her brain registered a newfound awareness of a woman's absolute power over the seemingly stronger sex.

She opened her lips under the caress of his, found her hands reaching up to Braille the rock sculpture of his cheekbones. She slid her hands from his cheekbones back into the thick waves of his dark, silken hair.

His lips continued to hold her captive, weaving some dark spell around her that seduced her senses and lured her into sharing a virgin part of herself with this man...this man, with whom, of all the men she had ever met, she wanted least to share these secrets of herself.

His lips compelled her to open her mouth yet wider beneath the command of his, to feel the soft lashing of his tongue within the private hollows of her own mouth. His tongue tasted like water cascading down the side of a mountain, fresh and clean beyond imagining. Pure.

Her hands slipped from his hair and tangled around his neck. She found herself pressing closer, needing to feel the hardness of that chest beneath the softness of her own breast. Needing to feel his maleness as a contrast to her femaleness. Aching for his touch as one might ache to plunge into deep, cold waters on a scorchingly hot desert afternoon.

His gentle plundering stopped, though his lips hovered near. She found herself opening her eyes, and looking at him with dazed longing.

If she had thought it weakened her, made her bones and her muscle turn to pudding, to be kissed, the absence of being kissed had an even more drugging, numbing effect. For a helpless moment she thought her knees might buckle.

But the cynical, knowing expression, mingled with the hunger in his eyes, brought her to her senses like a bucket of ice water tossed with ruthless insensitivity on an innocent sleeper.

She struggled proudly out of the grasp of the hard hands that held her upper arms. She glared at him warily.

"Hmm," he said with slow mockery. "Now that's my kind of *lady*." He turned from her, pulled his pants over his still damp shorts, and did up the zip without a trace of self-consciousness.

Those butterflies were storming *her* stomach again. She turned and marched away from him, something she should have done long ago.

She heard his soft and sensuous chuckle float on the moonbeams behind her.

She was shivering uncontrollably as she walked to her cabin. That man possessed an absolutely deadly charm—a charm that could make a prisoner of the most stalwart heart.

A deadly charm that could humiliate her because it could easily make her melt and beg and forget a lifetime of rigid adherence to propriety. And, damn his soul to hell, he knew it. He knew the exact drugging effect his potency had wreaked on her.

She thought of a wolf—silent, smart and terrifyingly strong—toying with its prey.

What on earth did Matthew Blake want with her?

CHARITY WOKE to a warbling voice singing happily. For a confused moment she felt as if it might be her own subconscious, ridiculously exhilarated by an encounter her intellect had found dreadful, humiliating and anxiety-provoking.

Well, she was a doctor, and she knew enough about human physiology to know that healthy men and women sometimes reacted to each other in the most devastating ways. All those wickedly powerful little hormones. The ticking of the biological clock.

The sun was blasting in her bedroom window and frolicking across her eyes. She groaned. She felt for all the world as if she had a hangover—an event that had happened exactly once in her well-ordered life.

"Mandy, what time is it?" she called.

Mandy waltzed in. "Going on noon."

"Noon?"

"It's okay. You worked hard. You'll need to lie in or you'll be too exhausted to have any fun."

"I'm too exhausted to have any fun right now," she said, sitting up and grumpily inspecting the blister between her small toe and the next one over.

"Was it awful?" Mandy asked sympathetically.

Charity grunted. "Your little joke didn't help."

"My joke?" Genuine puzzlement crossed Mandy's features and then they lit up with self-appreciation. "Oh, that. You really should have seen his face, love, it was quite priceless."

"I did see his face. And it wasn't priceless."

"You must learn to lighten up."

Charity dropped back into bed and pulled the pillow over her face. Smothering oneself was not an effective form of suicide, however. Besides, Mandy came over and started tickling her feet with a peacock plume she kept in a vase by the door.

"You have to get up. You said you wanted to come on my first canoe trip."

"I've changed my mind," Charity said, her voice muffled behind the pillow.

"You can't, love. I need you. We need pairs for the canoes and if you're a no-show we have a disappointed guest. Besides, last week that was one of the things you said you wanted to try out this summer."

"That was last week," she mumbled.

"And what do you want now?" Mandy asked cheerfully.

"To survive might be nice," Charity suggested.

An hour later, loaded down with awkward orange life jackets, she trailed her cousin down to the beach. After a while her weariness wore off. Mandy was a wonder to watch at work. She made the pre-canoe instructions absolutely hilarious, not to mention informative. She acted, she danced, she did imitations. She had those eager guests eating out of the palm of her hand in seconds.

Finally she assigned them into pairs.

Only there was no partner for Charity. By now she was awake enough to feel a stab of regret that she wouldn't be going out to glide over the surface of that calm blue water after all.

"Don't worry," Mandy said, seeing her expression. "He'll be here in a minute. I told him to take a miss on the instruction part. He's been canoeing for years. Oh, there he is now."

Charity turned to see Matthew Blake's tall, proud form coming toward her.

"Mandy!"

"Oh, don't use your surgeon-general voice on me. I'm not a scrub nurse."

"How could you?"

"You're perfect for each other," Mandy said firmly.

"Mandy, he already has this awful idea I'm chasing him. He'll think for sure I arranged this!"

"Well, so what? Have some fun with it. Flirt, for heaven's sake!"

"I don't want to flirt," she snapped. "I'd be safer flirting with a rattlesnake." This seemed to be falling on deaf ears. "*I* don't chase men."

"Time you learned," Mandy informed her with a disapproving cluck. "Now smile. You look as if you're about to cut someone's heart out."

Yours, Charity thought.

"Good afternoon, Lady Marlowe," a deep voice mocked her.

Or his.

"Good afternoon," she said tightly, which earned her a hard elbow in the ribs from Mandy.

"I've assigned you and Charity to a canoe together," Mandy said. Her voice was disgustingly close to gushing. "Charity said she'd like to get to know you better."

"My, my," he said, raising one eyebrow wickedly at her.

"That's not what I said!" She could feel her face flushing. Mandy had the utter audacity to roll her eyes coyly at Matthew.

Charity knew that to protest anymore would only undermine her credibility. She had to satisfy herself with biting her lip and plotting revenge on that redheaded menace who was always disrupting somebody's life.

Meanwhile, she had the whole afternoon to prove to Mr. All-too-sure-of-himself Blake that she knew exactly how to behave like a lady. He would never again witness reserve and decorum as he was about to witness.

"You seem rather shy today," he said as she stood stiffly facing the lake, ignoring him. There was a teasing note to his voice.

"That's not shyness," she said stuffily. "It's reserve."

"Ladylike reserve?" he guessed, an aggravating hint of laughter in his voice.

"Exactly."

"People with ladylike reserve generally don't go swimming in the buff in public places, but—"

"If you are going to discuss last night, I am not going to go!"

"After all the trouble you went to to arrange this?"

"I did not arrange this!" she said huffily. "I did not do—"

"Well, there goes the reserve," he said, amicably enough. "And good riddance, too."

"I *am* reserved."

"Show me," he said, with that faint and familiar glittering challenge in his eyes.

That was exactly where things had gone awry last night, and she wasn't falling into that trap again.

"I don't think I'll go canoeing after all," she said stiffly. "I seem to be developing a headache."

A strong hand caught her elbow. "Just get in the boat, Lady Marlowe."

"Quit calling me that." Her elbow was tingling where he was touching it. "Let go of my arm."

"I'm just helping you into the canoe. A lady like you should appreciate such a gentlemanly gesture."

"I hate you." She could not believe such an entirely childish phrase had popped out of her mouth.

Matthew laughed. "It is not appropriate for staff members to put guests at the center of...*scenes.*"

Scenes, indeed, she huffed to herself. The ego of this man knew no limits. Did he think people watched him? Monitored his every move? Did he think he was so wonderfully interesting that—

Out of the corner of her eyes, she caught the fact that they *were* being stared at with unveiled interest by most members of the group, the most curious of all, of course, being Mandy. Color flared in her cheeks. She was aware of a strange electrical current humming in the air between herself and Matthew Blake, and she realized that that current was causing curiosity.

The only way she knew how to dispel it was to break free of his grasp and get into the canoe. Anpetuwi was small—a breeding ground for gossip, and she'd probably end up regretting it if she turned and walked up that hill.

She got in the canoe so rapidly that she nearly tipped it over. She fully intended to give Matthew Blake the most miserable afternoon of company he had ever had! That should put a swift end to these weird undercurrents that danced between them.

She knelt on her knees, as Mandy had explained, resting her haunches against the wooden seat. She felt the boat accept his weight—without nearly tipping—but she refused to look back over her shoulder at him. She burned some of her angry energy in the pure physical release of putting that paddle into the water and pulling hard against the resisting force.

They had been paddling in tension-filled silence for some time when he spoke. "What does Char stand for?"

She refused to speak.

"Charlotte?"

She said nothing, surveying the landscape with cool hauteur. She'd pretend he was the servant, obediently paddling her down the Nile. She sneaked a look over her shoulder at him. Unfortunately he looked more the warrior-who-would-kidnap-a-bride type than a docile servant.

A sardonic lip twisted upward. "Charissa?"

"I'm not telling."

"At least you're speaking. Charla?"

"I am under no obligation to tell you my name, Mr. Blake."

"Matthew."

"I prefer Mr. Blake."

"It's a little late for formality."

"No, it isn't."

The faintest flicker of humor could be heard in his voice. "I do get mixed messages from you—Charleen? I don't know whether to believe those eyes are really innocent or if the innocence is one of those confusing invitations your sex is so fond of."

"Ah," she said, slow understanding dawning in her voice. "You've had a run-in with one of my sex, haven't you?" She rested her paddle and glanced over her shoulder at him. "Recently."

She could see, now, something she had not seen before. What seemed like arrogance might be wariness. Wariness that masked a hurt.

But all the friendliness his teasing tone had indicated was gone from his face. Now, it was chiseled into remote lines, his eyes a shade slightly cooler than a glacier.

"I'm not her," she said softly.

"Nobody said you were," he said coolly. She realized he could teach her a thing or two about reserve. And she also realized that it was not her job to heal the hurts of the whole world—though certainly her very nature leaned in that direction.

Still, a person would be a fool to go after something as dangerous as a wounded wolf armed only with sympathy.

Besides which, sympathy was not the feeling this potently masculine man she was sharing this canoe with stirred in her. It was a feeling far less civilized than that. Something primal, which she couldn't quite put her finger on.

She chose to ignore him again, paddling on in silence, not knowing if the tension in her shoulders was from the unfamiliar strain of the exercise or from the unfamiliar strain of having eyes probe one's back with habitual cynicism.

"You still haven't told me your name."

She stopped, and looked back at him. He knelt easily, powerful arms moving smoothly with the paddle, his face, in profile to her as he studied something on shore, rugged and uncaring. But, when he met her eyes, for a moment there was a flicker of some deep pain in his eyes.

"My name is Charity," she gave in.

He almost flinched and then a sardonic smile twisted his lips. "It suits you," he admitted harshly. "Purity, innocence. But I sense a lie about you, too. Something that doesn't add up. It makes me uneasy."

"Just let me jump out of the canoe for you," she muttered through gritted teeth, returning to paddling with a new fury.

Mandy had planned a short trip: about a forty-five-minute paddle and then a stop for lunch at a secluded bay down the lake, and then back.

Between his strength and her anger, she and Matthew had pulled up well in the lead of other canoes.

It came so fast that she hardly knew what had happened. Mandy had warned her that storms came up fast on the lake, but nothing could have prepared her for blue skies being annihilated by black storm clouds in just a matter of minutes. The water went from calm to storm-tossed and the canoe began to jog sickeningly.

"Keep it into the waves," Matthew shouted. "As long as the waves don't start hitting into the sides of the canoe we won't be swamped."

The wind was lifting his hair, and he looked wild and untamed and . . . wonderful. He looked in charge, and challenged by the storm. To her horror he slowly turned the canoe out into the lake instead of in to shore. Even then, she didn't feel afraid. She had dealt with enough crisis situations that she was very slow to panic, but she realized something else. Her feelings about this man might be ambiguous to the point of causing insanity, but she became acutely aware of something. If she was on a plane with the engines on fire she would want to be with someone like Matthew Blake.

"I want to make sure the others are safely on shore," he shouted above the rising roar of the storm.

In a moment, they were far enough out that they could see miles down the rocky shoreline...and they could see the other boaters scrambling up onto a piece of rock. Mandy spotted them and waved that they were all right, and Matthew turned and headed them into a safe cove, too.

He turned the canoe back in, using the full power of those arms to bring them rapidly toward shore.

They spent the next few minutes getting themselves and the canoe off the water.

"It's only a thundershower," Matthew said calmly, looking out at the storm-tossed lake. "It's magnificent, isn't it?"

She glimpsed the magnificence then, in both the lake and in him. She didn't want him to be a man with *any* redeeming qualities. She didn't want him to be able to appreciate thunderstorms. She didn't want him to worry about the safety of their fellow travelers. She didn't want him to have a hurt heart that he hid with bitter repartee. It made him seem altogether too human, and the safest thing for her to do would be to remember that this man was very nearly the devil incarnate.

"We'll be back on the lake in an hour. Let's find a nice dry place, have our lunch, and watch the storm."

Charity looked at the sky. A bolt of lightning ripped it open, and the light was followed closely by a deep rumble of thunder.

She knew Matthew Blake was the sort of man who didn't make mistakes often, but he was wrong this time. The storm was not going to blow itself out in an hour—not even for him.

And she had the uneasy feeling that the stormy feelings between them weren't going to blow themselves out, either. Not in an hour. Not in a day. Perhaps not even in the long summer that stretched ahead of them.

She could see the thunderheads building all along the edges of her one perfect summer, and she shivered apprehensively.

CHAPTER FOUR

"THIS LOOKS LIKE as good a spot as any," Matthew decided. He was carrying a huge wicker basket, provided by the lodge for a snack. He led the way under a huge Ponderosa pine. The branches dipped nearly to the ground, but when Charity ducked in she found a cozy hollow underneath the tree that seemed dry and snug as a little house. The rich scent of the tree was intensified by the rain.

"What if this tree gets hit by lightning?" she asked, peering up and up through the twisted branches.

Matthew laughed, a low mocking sound. "Then I guess you and I are toast, my dear. Some things have to be left to fate."

He shook out the blanket that topped the picnic items, and sat, his back against the trunk, those long legs stretched out in front of him. Though she would have been more comfortable beside him, with her back against the tree, she didn't want to risk touching him. She chose to sit cross-legged in front of him, then decided that wasn't exactly a good choice either. The moisture had made his hair curl even more, and had brought out the hardiness of his complexion.

Outside their refuge the rain began to come down in earnest.

Matthew peered with interest into the basket.

"At least they do this right," he murmured. He began to unpack a delightful array of items—including two one-serving-size bottles of wine.

She felt herself prickle at his tone. Where had her strong sense of loyalty to Anpetuwi come from?

"They do *this* right?" she probed. "Meaning you aren't that happy with your stay at Anpetuwi?"

"There have been a few problems," he said flatly.

"It's only your third day here!"

"Exactly," he said dryly.

"Perhaps you're very hard to please," she said. "The lodge doesn't pretend to be in competition with more sophisticated places."

"It charges the same prices," he pointed out.

"What you are paying for is a total experience, and for the setting. Perhaps you should try some place more in keeping with your personality!"

He seemed unoffended, though his eyes had narrowed thoughtfully on her. "And where might you suggest, Miss Marlowe?"

She wanted to suggest that he might be very happy having his vacation in hell, but decided that anywhere halfway round the world would do!

"How about the French Riviera? You could gamble at night and enjoy nude beaches during the day."

"Is that the type I strike you as?"

"Yes. You do seem to enjoy watching nude bathers, so don't you think it would be much better for everyone involved if you went somewhere where they didn't mind being watched?"

A trace of a smile touched those hard lips. "Maybe it's *you* who should be on the French Riviera."

"Do you suppose they need a not-so-hot cocktail waitress there?" she said, somewhat flippantly.

"Probably not," he said dryly.

She wished she wasn't offended that he didn't rush to assure her that she wasn't that bad a waitress.

"Anyway," she said firmly, "I think Anpetuwi is charming just the way it is. I wouldn't change one thing about it."

"It seems to be a staff paradise, all right."

"What a cynical thing to say. The fact that the staff members like working at Anpetuwi is part of its charm. I personally think you must be a very unhappy man if you have to go to such lengths to find fault with things."

"Would you care to change my unhappy status?" he asked suavely. He winked wickedly at her.

She decided she wasn't going to be thrown off by his attempt to annoy her.

"Mr. Blake," she said quietly, "I can't make you happy. And all the money and Mercedeses in the world can't do it either. Anpetuwi can't make you happy. That particular commodity is something you find in the far reaches of your own soul—and if you haven't got it, the reason is also within you—not me or Anpetuwi."

A puzzled light lit his eyes, then was quickly hooded. "That was very profound," he said, quietly, but then refused to be drawn into a more serious mood. "The waitress philosopher strikes again."

She realized she was being too serious, a problem that had plagued her all her life. She didn't know how to be light. She didn't know how to banter with the opposite sex. She turned, suddenly uneasy in his company, so that she wasn't facing him anymore, and watched the stormy lake.

"How old are you, Charity?"

"How old do you think I am?" she asked evasively.

"You look to be nineteen or twenty, but sometimes the way you talk makes me think you're older."

"You're right. I'm older."

"How much older?" he probed.

"I'm going to exercise my woman's prerogative," she said firmly. If he knew how old she was he might want her to tell him what she had been doing the last few years.

"I'll guess twenty-three."

"That's a good guess," she said, neither denying it nor confirming it.

"So what do you do in your other life, when you're not at Anpetuwi?"

She had known that sooner or later she would be asked that. Mandy had advised her, blithely, to lie. But she wasn't a good liar, and it was not a talent she was particularly interested in cultivating.

"What makes you think I'm not a full-time career waitress?"

"You said it yourself—you're not so hot at it."

"Oh." She felt ridiculously deflated, even though his assessment only matched her own.

"So, *if* you're in your early twenties you've been out of high school for several years. What have you been doing?"

"I'll tell you what—if you guess correctly, I'll tell you."

"All right," he agreed amiably. He studied her thoughtfully. "You're beautiful, and it would make it easy to guess you were a receptionist for a high-powered company. The kind who sits in a little island in the middle of a highly polished marble floor, looking gorgeous and untouchable, but..."

"I don't look gorgeous and untouchable," she said with a snort.

"We'll settle for just gorgeous, then," he agreed, something faintly heated entering his eyes, though his voice remained casual. "But somehow the receptionist thing doesn't fit, any more than your being a waitress does."

"Umm," she said nervously.

"You're tall and you carry yourself extremely well. It makes me think of models."

"Models? Me?" she said, looking at him with wide eyes. Matthew Blake certainly seemed to see a Charity Marlowe that nobody else had ever seen. Except Mandy. And Mandy, darn her hide, had coaxed it out so the whole world could see it. Unfortunately it was making Charity feel like a stranger in her own skin.

"Not a model. All right. It didn't sit well, anyway."

What wasn't sitting well was those sapphire eyes studying her with such disturbing intensity that she felt stripped to her soul!

"That turn of phrase you have... would seem to indicate a good deal of education."

She kept her face carefully blank.

"A teacher? That's what your cousin does the rest of the year, isn't it? And it would explain your having several months off. It makes sense, but it doesn't quite fit. I can't picture you surrounded by thirty children with adoration in their eyes."

"I happen to like children very much!"

"I didn't say you didn't. I simply said I couldn't picture you doing anything as unglamorous as helping wee ones count to ten."

If he wanted unglamorous, he should see what she looked like in surgical greens after about twelve hours in the OR, though, of course, she couldn't even hint at that.

"I think I won't repeat this conversation to Mandy," Charity muttered. "Besides, I could teach older children, couldn't I?"

"You could, but I'll bet you don't. You haven't developed the icy crust a beautiful woman who daily battles off the advances of adolescent boys would have."

And here she had thought she was doing admirably in the icy crust department!

Matthew must have read her mind, because he laughed. "I have nothing but respect for teachers. I just don't see you being challenged by it. And you do something challenging, don't you, Miss Mystery Marlowe?"

That, from Mr. Mystery himself?

"I didn't know the meaning of the word 'challenge' until my first night of slinging drinks in the Susweca," she said, giving him nothing, and taking great satisfaction in it, too.

He laughed again. She wished he'd stop it. It made him unforgivably attractive with the laugh lines creasing at the sides of his eyes, and those strong white teeth flashing in the dimness. When he stopped laughing the boyish expression lingered compelling on his face.

"I'll figure out who you are. I'm extremely good at this kind of game."

She suspected he *was* extremely good at this kind of game—this was the kind of game men and women played together. Flirtatious. And dangerous. She was way out of her league and she knew it.

"It might take me all summer, but I'll do it. Something glamorous and challenging. Like racing cars, except I detect a missing element of boldness. When I figure out what you do, you won't even have to confirm it. I'll just know—the light will go off in my head. Now it's your turn."

"I'm not good at games," she said uneasily.

"You told your cousin you wanted to get to know me better," he reminded her.

"I didn't actually say that."

"What actually did you say?" His tone was smooth and teasing, but his eyes were glittering with a disturbing light.

Much as Mandy's well-intentioned little white lies annoyed her, Charity felt intensely loyal to her irrepressible cousin, and she wasn't going to tell him that Mandy had an unfortunate trait of bending the truth into whatever pigeonholes suited her.

"I don't remember what I actually said, but obviously Mandy misinterpreted it in some way. Mandy does that." It was as close as she could come to the truth without feeling disloyal.

"Take a guess," he encouraged her, his tone light. "We have nothing but time. The rain isn't letting up."

Since he put it that way, like a parlor game, intended to keep him from dying of boredom in her company, which was more the effect she was used to having on men, she considered.

"You're a high-powered businessman, though I can't guess the business."

"You're close. What gave me away?"

"Either the Mercedes or the silk shirts."

"So why not a lawyer or a doctor or an accountant?"

"You're too ruthless to be a doctor, not sly enough to be a lawyer, and not boring enough to be an accountant."

"I don't consider myself ruthless."

"The ruthless never do."

"At least I can be flattered that you don't find me sly or boring."

"What difference does it make to you how I find you?"

"I don't know. But it does."

She felt uneasy again, some electricity beginning to leap in the air between their locked eyes. She looked away first, and pawed through the wicker basket, looking for something to fill the space between them. She found some large pieces of cake, and thrust one at him.

He unwrapped it, and sniffed it. "What do you suppose this cake has in it?"

From animosity, to electricity, to discussing cake ingredients in the blink of an eye.

"I haven't a clue," she retorted, "but it's wonderful."

He set his piece aside.

She understood immediately. "Do you have an allergy?"

He didn't seem very pleased at her perception. Men, she thought impatiently, took even the smallest things as a sign of weakness.

"I don't get along very well with almonds. I thought there might be a trace in the cake."

"Do you have a severe allergic reaction?"

"Even a small amount could kill me if I wasn't within minutes of medical care."

She was relieved he wasn't taking any chances. If he had an anaphylactic reaction out here, there would be nothing she could do to help him, doctor or not. He'd need adrenalin right into the vein and she didn't have a medical kit with her.

"So, now you know what to do if I ever make you angry enough. I lay this sword at your feet, fair maiden."

Unfortunately her oath precluded her ever being able to use it.

They polished off the rest of the snack—luscious fresh fruit—in silence. Though she rarely drank, Charity drained her small bottle of wine, hoping for some small illusion of warmth from it. The shelter underneath the tree no longer seemed as cozy. The dampness was coming in, and she was dressed only in a thin T-shirt and shorts.

"Maybe we could light a fire," she suggested, looking briefly up at him, and feeling somewhat disconcerted at the way those eyes were resting on her. She quickly changed her position, so that she was no longer facing him but looking out toward the lake.

"And with what shall we light it, dear Liza?"

"One of those matches that you use on those filthy things you smoke."

"Have you noticed me smoking one of those filthy things?"

"As a matter of fact, I haven't."

"I haven't had one since your little lecture on my lungs, actually."

She turned startled eyes to him. "Really?"

"Really. You should bottle that particular speech and sell it to clean-air groups."

She allowed herself a small smile, mostly because he'd accepted her medical opinion but still hadn't guessed she was a doctor. And hopefully never would, she reminded herself. It was easy, somehow, to be drawn into his game, though she would do well to remind herself that it was very likely nothing about Matthew Blake was innocent.

"I'm not sure I'd light a fire if I had a match," he continued. "I've never seen this area this dry this early in the year."

"It's not dry now," she pointed out.

"It would probably take a week of rain like this to reduce the forest-fire hazard."

She felt puzzled and once again turned and looked at him. "For a man hailing from London, England, you seem to be familiar with the forest situation in the Okanagan."

"I grew up here." He said this softly, and with faint hesitation. It made her very aware that he didn't want to give up any information about himself...and especially not to her.

But maybe that explained, a bit, why he was here. He was a hard, cold, cynical man who had let himself be hurt by a woman. She'd be willing to put money on that. And somehow his hurt had brought him back here, looking for some innocence long since gone from him, looking for some boyhood simplicity to answer the anguish within him, to make it go away.

So they both were searching for some lost part of themselves this summer.

The rain continued. Except for the steady drum of drops, the wind in the trees and the waves slapping angrily at rock, there was silence. When she glanced back at him he seemed comfortable with the silence, watching the rain and the lake, his blue eyes, not so different in color from that storm-tossed lake, appreciative and thoughtful.

"Charity, you're shivering. Are you cold?"

"Not really," she lied proudly.

"Come here. We'll wrap this blanket around us." He pulled the blanket from underneath himself and draped it over his shoulders.

"Not on your life," she muttered through trembling teeth.

"Come here before you catch a cold, you stubborn little minx."

"You don't catch colds from being cold," she informed him. "You catch colds from a virus." She brought her knees up to her chest and wrapped her goose-bumped arms around them.

Strong arms reached around her from behind. He settled one hand on each side of her hips and pulled her back into the V of his legs. His arms slid upward, until his hair-roughened, powerful forearms stopped and crossed just beneath her breasts. The blanket settled over her shoulders and around her cold bare arms.

She wanted to struggle against him with all her might. But his warmth crept into her and seduced her. His chest was broad and hard behind her head. His chin rested on the top of her hair, and his breath stirred its tendrils. She felt safe and warm and oddly happy. She felt tired from the unexpected strain of this afternoon. Her eyelids drooped, fluttered, and then drooped again. With a small sigh of surrender she fell asleep in the arms of a man she didn't understand, and wanted very badly to detest.

She awoke aware of four things—it was dark; the rain had stopped; her T-shirt had pulled up and strong, warm arms rested protectively on her midriff; and the back of her was very warm and the front of her was very cold. Sleepily she tried to adjust for this situation, flipping over and snuggling into the heated surface of his chest.

"Isn't this just about where we left off?" His voice was husky and dark, like part of the night. One of his hands wrapped in her hair, while the other, resting on her back, pulled her tighter into him. Her breasts were crushed flat against the wall of his chest. She could feel the tremors of his heart go from a steady pounding to something more erratic.

"Left off?" she murmured sleepily.

"Last night."

"Oh." She made a halfhearted effort to pull away from him, but ran into the implacable strength of his arm. She contented herself with pulling the T-shirt down over her bare stomach.

He chuckled, and too late she caught the wicked note to it. Her eyes flew open just as his lips found the delicate curve of her neck. A spasm of delight shook her from head to toe as he plundered her neck. Then those lips moved with agonizing delight to her ears.

"Matthew," she whispered as another tremor shuddered through her. "Don't."

"All right," he said, "I won't." But he did. He shifted under her, sliding her away so that she was still bound to him by the steel bands of his arms, but was now lying by his side. A muscular leg came up and trapped hers beneath it.

She squirmed, but only until his lips brushed hers.

He lifted his head and looked down at her, his eyes unholy, his hand moving up her rib cage with slow deliberation. He stopped just short of the swell of her breast.

"You...said...you...wouldn't," she breathed, her eyes wide.

"I know," he whispered, and a smile flitted across the devastatingly handsome cast of his face. "I lied."

His hand circled around the fullness of her breast, and he squeezed with a gentle possessiveness that did violence to her breathing. He lowered his head and kissed the taut peak where it strained against the thin fabric of her T-shirt.

"Matthew—" she gasped. It sounded, even to her, more like a plea than a protest.

"Shh." Warm hands spanned her rib cage, and worked the fabric of her shirt slowly upward. Fire danced in his eyes as the cool night air hit her naked breast.

"Charity, you are incredibly beautiful."

She was losing her battle with her senses. They were swamping her, obliterating her better judgment. His tongue flicked the nub of her nipple, circled her breast languorously and then flicked again.

She wanted to stop him, but she found him totally irresistible. The chemistry had been between them from the start, waiting only for a wayward spark to ignite it. Now it was blazing steadily, promising an out-of-control inferno, unless she came to her senses and stopped it.

Her breath was coming in hard, hot gasps. She tried to make herself think rationally. What did she know about this man, really? What did . . . ? Her hands had moved under his shirt and found satisfaction in the sultry silk of his skin. She touched him with a hunger she had not known she harbored inside her. She reveled in the feeling of hard male flesh beneath her fingertips. She kneaded his back, and touched the plane of his belly, and explored the hard, sinewy mounds of his arms.

In these moments of gilded sensuality she had the wonderful feeling that she knew everything she needed to know, right here, and right now, right beneath her fingertips.

He lifted his head from her breast and scanned her face. With a moan of utter and ecstatic defeat she twined her arms around his neck and pulled those sensuous lips onto her own mouth.

Her lips opened eagerly beneath his, and her tongue darted out to trace the contours of his mouth, feeling the silk of his upper lip and the fullness of his lower one. Growing bolder, she made a dash into the hollow of his mouth, and touched his teeth, played briefly with his tongue, before darting back out.

She heard him moan, low in his throat, a sound somewhere between pain and delight. She traced the line of his cheekbone with her tongue, up to his ear. She tasted it and nibbled on it, and plunged into it, until a hand took her chin and their mouths once again met.

She became aware that he was tracing the line of her breast with one hand, and that ever so lightly he was scraping his palm against her erect nipple.

The fingers of his other hand beat a sensuous tattoo on her rounded bottom, stopping to tap and then sweeping away the notes with a furious stroke.

"Lift up your arms," he whispered, his teeth gnawing tenderly at her ear.

Mutely she complied, and in a smooth movement he had stripped her T-shirt from her. In one more smooth movement his own shirt was gone, and as she looked at him her naked skin seemed to cry out for the touch of his.

He lowered himself onto her breasts and she moaned as he held himself up on his elbows and barely allowed himself to touch her, his hard chest sliding lightly back and forth over the aching tenderness of her bosom.

She locked her arms around the small of his back and pulled him hard into her, crazed by the sensation caused by his utter maleness enveloping her softness.

And when she had thought sensation could not go any higher or wider or further, he touched her lightly and tenderly in the vulnerable V between her legs. When she arched wildly against him, he cupped his hand there, and she felt the heat of his wanting in his fingertips.

She heard the zip of her shorts being drawn down, and he dropped his head to place a tender, almost welcoming kiss on her silken mound. He tossed her shorts away, then sat up and looked at her with desire-darkened eyes as he tugged down the zip on his own shorts and flung them away.

They were naked now, in the soft cradle of the tree. The stars blinked, somewhere out there, and the night air was cold against her flesh—a cold that could be chased away almost immediately by the white-hot intensity of his heat.

His fingers found her most sensitive spot and touched with feather lightness again and again, until she was wriggling against him, her hair sticking wildly around her face.

"Do you want me?" he whispered.

She stared at him. At his rugged face, shadowed by darkness, into the unearthly blue of his eyes. The words came from deep within her. For once her formidable intellect was not in charge. Something else, wilder, uninhibited, even more formidable than her mind, was completely in charge. Her heart answered him.

"Yes," she whispered. "I want you."

Gently he parted her legs, and held himself above her. For a moment he searched her face, looking for something, and then he seemed to find it, whatever he was searching for, for with a half smile, his eyes still open and fixed on her face, he entered her.

He was incredibly strong and she closed her legs around him, driven by some instinct to try and pull him deeper within her. He rose and then dived within her, starting slowly as if to the beating of a primal drum.

Then faster and faster, as she rose to be joined with him in every sense of the word.

They plunged over the very edge of the human capacity to feel. They did not feel sensation, but *became* sensation, pulsating, thrilling, climbing, soaring, diving, and then falling back toward earth only to soar suddenly upward again.

A cry, pure and primal, came from her lips, and was followed by deep shudders of sensation that felt like the very earth trembling.

They lay, joined, for a long time, their breath coming in rapid gasps, their sweat filming their skin with sensuality, their eyes locked together in some unbelievable acknowledgment of each other.

She reached out and touched his face with her fingertips, but it seemed to break whatever spell they had been under.

"Charity," he said, his voice choked. "Oh, Charity, what have we done?"

It felt to her as if they had just unlocked the key to the whole universe, but she had a feeling that was not what he meant. There was something in his face and eyes she did not like—a softness that seemed almost like sympathy.

She felt stunned. She could feel tears beginning to clog at her throat and make the area behind her eyes sting.

"Don't cry," he said softly.

"I wasn't going to," she said, with a furious attempt for dignity.

"Charity, why didn't you tell me?"

"Tell you what?"

"That it was your first time?"

She stared at him. If she had been rational enough to tell him something it certainly wouldn't have been that. It would have been stop!

She sat up and tugged her shirt over the hopeless tangle of her hair. She groped around for her panties and shorts, ducking her head to put them on so that he wouldn't see the tears gathering in the corners of her eyes.

This was not what she had expected—or wanted. How could this have happened in her well-ordered life? Somewhere in the back of her mind she had thought there would be champagne and strawberries and maybe silk sheets. And love. Definitely love.

"Don't shut me out," he commanded softly.

"I didn't want that to happen."

"All right," he said, "I wasn't planning it either."

"I was trying to convince you this was the kind of girl I wasn't," she said dully.

"You convinced me," he said softly. "You should have told me, Charity. I don't know how, but somehow I would have stopped."

"I'm late for work and it's only my second night."

That look of sympathy deepened in his eyes, as if he knew she was just casting around desperately to try and outrun the turmoil of her own feelings.

"Why me?" he asked softly.

What did he want her to say? Because he was so devilishly attractive that she couldn't resist him? Because there was something in his eyes that had beckoned to her? Because his arms had felt as good around her as anything had ever felt in her life? Because his lips had opened a brand-new world up to her? A world of dizzying sensation where she had never been before? What did he want her to say?

"Why you? Why not? It had to be somebody." She said this flatly, hiding all the emotion she felt.

She had just lost something she could never get back. She was a doctor. She knew medically what had happened to her. She knew it was a modern world and that it happened to people all the time and that it wasn't such a big deal—medically or culturally.

Still, she felt as if she should feel... some remorse. And she didn't. Confusion, certainly. But not remorse.

It had been perfect, so much more than she had ever imagined this act could be. But she couldn't let him see that it had *meant* something to her. That might intensify that odd look of sympathy on his face, as if he already *knew* it meant something to her, when it meant nothing to him.

"I don't know what the future holds," he said softly.

"The immediate future holds several hours of waitressing for me," she said with a brittle brightness that didn't seem to fool him. "In an hour I'll be passing out drinks."

"Charity, let me hold you."

"No!"

"I'm sorry."

How could she tell him that was the worst thing he could say? How could he be *sorry?*

"There's no need to apologize. We're two adults. These things happen between adults."

His mouth twisted wryly. "Well, obviously you're one adult it doesn't happen to. Didn't."

"Could we just go? The water looks quite calm. I—"

"Charity, we can't pretend it didn't happen."

Watch me, she thought.

"I feel as if you've given me a gift I'm completely unworthy of. Things are not settled in my life right now, Charity."

"Nobody's asking you to marry me," she said stiffly. She gathered all her strength around her. "In fact, I think it might be better if we tried not to have any more contact with each other, don't you?"

He looked at her with troubled eyes, but she could not know how much his answer was going to hurt.

"I suppose that might be better. Nearly impossible, given the circumstances, but better."

She wasn't sure what he meant by "circumstances." The fact that they would both be at Anpetuwi for the summer? Or the fact that the chemistry between them just wouldn't stop?

Already her body was craving his again, longing for the strength of his arms, for the hard rhythm of his taking her.

Suddenly, she knew what she had to do. She preferred the sizzling animosity between them to this...this awkwardness. She wanted to erase forever the faint concern etched into the darkness of his brow as he watched her, his gaze unrelenting, seeming to see into her soul.

He was looking at her as if he was wondering, will she be all right? Will she try and make more of this than it was?

She had to salvage her pride, forsake forever the tenderness that ached within her for this man....

With a devil-may-care laugh, she bounced to her feet, scooped up her shoes and raced toward the water.

Gasping with desperate exertion, she got the canoe into the water, and leapt into it just as he seemed to realize what she was doing.

She shoved the canoe out into the water with a paddle.

"Charity!"

She ignored him.

"Come back here!"

Again she ignored him, doing amazingly well at steering the canoe out into the still waters of the lake. The moon blazed her trail home.

Tears streaking down her face, she acknowledged the irony of it. The landscape—the moon on dark water, and the rugged shoreline—was as romantic as she had ever seen it.

And she had just made love to a stranger. And the worst part of it was that it had been so wonderful that it would be hard to avoid doing it again.

But she had her fair share of steel in her makeup, and she made a vow to herself which echoed eerily down the lonesome length of the lake.

"Never again, Matthew Blake. Never."

She managed to smile through her tears. Matthew Blake was going to be so hopping mad that, the next time he saw her, making love would be the last thing on his mind!

CHAPTER FIVE

"YOU LOOK simply gorgeous."

Charity knew that was true. She had raced up to her cabin wondering how she was going to repair herself enough to put in the rest of her shift. She'd been amazed to see that the effects of the tears barely showed.

What had showed was high color in her cheeks, and a candlelike light glowing deep in the back of her eyes.

"Thank you, Nelson, and thank you for taking over my shift."

She'd been amazed to see Nelson working for her—and even more amazed to see how good he was at it, laughing and chatting with the customers, apparently having the time of his life.

She found herself wishing they could trade permanently. She could drive the golf cart and he could wait on tables.

"I didn't exactly do it for nothing," Nelson said. He inexpertly raised an eyebrow at her.

"Of course, I'd be happy to pay you for your time." She began to count her float.

"Pay me?" he yelped with youthful offence. "I don't want your money!"

Charity glanced up at him.

"I want you to go for dinner with me."

She didn't suppose the timing could be any worse. But she also didn't see any way she could graciously say no after Nelson had just saved her bacon.

Besides, he was funny and youthful, the opposite pole to Matthew Blake. Maybe she had better start planning relentlessly to fill her spare moments so she had no time to think.

"All right," she said with a smile.

"You won't be sorry. I'm a great guy."

"I know that," she told him kindly. "Only a really special person would help out someone they barely knew like this."

Nelson beamed, and went on his way.

Her shift passed rapidly, and, though her heart fluttered every time someone walked in the door of the lounge, it was never a wet, muddy, and very angry Matthew Blake.

She dragged herself up the hill to find that Mandy was still awake, reading a book in bed by the light of her kerosene bedside lamp. A green mud mask was smeared on her face.

"I thought you'd be sleeping," she said to her cousin.

"Are you kidding? I want all the details."

"What details?"

"A boy and girl in a little canoe," Mandy sang happily.

"What are you talking about?"

"It's a campfire song. It ends with her making a decision to kiss him or get out and swim. So, which was it?"

"I don't suppose 'none of your business' is going to do much good, is it?" She had tried to sound breezy, but her voice cracked, and she turned swiftly away from the sudden concern in Mandy's big green eyes.

Mandy got out of bed and touched her shoulder. "Char, what happened?"

"I don't want to talk about it."

"Either you tell me, or I'll march right over to his room and ask him."

Charity turned and faced her cousin. There was grim determination in every line of that elfin face.

"So help me, if he hurt you—"

"Mandy, stop it. I'm a grown woman. I can take care of myself."

"No, you can't. For heaven's sake, you've been breathing the rarefied air of the ivory tower for as long as I can remember. You don't know the first thing about real life."

A sob caught in Charity's throat. It wasn't true. She'd seen more of life and death at twenty-six than most people would see in their entire lifetime. And yet it was true, too.

"He made love to you, didn't he?"

"Mandy! That's none of your business!" But the tears started to come hard and fast.

"That scoundrel! I'm going to—"

"Mandy! You are going to do nothing."

Mandy was already at the door, slipping on shoes. Mindless of the fact she was in a flannel nightie, and had a green face, she looked quite prepared to go slay the dragon.

"He isn't here."

"Where is he?" she snapped, her tone suggesting that she was prepared to track him down.

"I took the canoe and left him there."

"Good for you. Boy, am I going to give him a piece of my mind when I see him. An experienced, worldly guy like that—"

"Mandy, stop it. It's between him and me. And I'm twenty-six years old. I don't need you to go to bat for me."

Mandy hesitated and then a smile softened her face. "Hey, that's right, isn't it? You know, I've always felt protective of you. Do you remember the time I blacked Tom Bellinger's eye for calling you a 'Four-eyed freak'? I hated that when people picked on you. I wanted everybody to see how wonderful you were, even though you were so different from the rest of us."

Charity was relieved that she seemed to have managed to sidetrack Mandy. "That's what I remember most about my childhood. Being different. Not being able to communicate with my peers."

"Yeah, you just don't find ten-year-old children who can discuss Shakespeare, do you?"

"I always felt as if you rode in on a white charger and saved me from my loneliness. In all the world, you were the one who loved me and accepted me exactly as I was. Thanks, Mandy."

Mandy, her battle lust having died down as quickly as it had set in, flopped down on Charity's bed, and patted the spot beside her.

"So, since I don't have to go give him a hard one in the chops, tell me about it. Was it great?"

"Mandy, for Pete's sake!" There was no such thing as sidetracking a one-track mind.

"It's no crime to be curious!"

Charity couldn't help but laugh. "Okay, it was great. And awful, and I've never been so confused in my whole life."

"That sounds just about normal. So, Doc, did you use birth control?"

Charity sighed. This was a bad moment for her. As a doctor, she, of all people, should have known better. "No. It... just happened."

"Nothing ever comes of it the first time, anyway," Mandy assured her.

"Mandy, I have to tell you, medically, that is complete nonsense."

"Well, look at it this way, then. There you are out innocently canoeing, with the most gorgeous man this side of the Rocky Mountains, and out of nowhere a storm hits. What are the chances of that happening? One in a thousand? I mean, you are practically forced into a close encounter, and nobody could miss the electricity between the two of you. Even then, the chances of *that* happening were probably about one in a thousand, again. Then, what are the chances of getting pregnant? I mean they must be one in a thousand, too, aren't they?"

"Not quite that high," Charity said glumly.

"Even so, if the rabbit died, I think you could take it as fate's plan for you. I really do."

"Thank you, Mandy, that would certainly help me come to terms with all my shattered dreams. Could you get out of my bed now? I'd like to go to sleep."

"Who knows?" Mandy got off the bed, and stretched. "Maybe you were dreaming the wrong dreams for you. Maybe fate had to give you a shove onto the right path."

"That's a deep thought, coming from someone with a bright green face," Charity teased. She found her pajamas. "You know, Mandy, I think you could find a bright spot in the middle of the black hole."

"I'd certainly try," Mandy agreed, hopping into her own bed, and pulling the covers up around her green chin. "Boy, am I ever glad I've got a front-row seat for this. Charity's first romance!"

"It is not my *first* romance."

"Oh, do tell," Mandy said with disbelief.

"I was madly in love with a guy in med school. His name was Jeff Warner."

"Really? What happened?"

"We studied together. We worked together. We even grabbed lunch together a few times at the hospital cafeteria."

"Sounds pretty hot all right," Mandy noted callously.

"We were friends. We talked about everything and anything. I thought that might make a pretty sound basis for a partnership of a different kind."

"Uh-oh," Mandy interjected, with a sad little shake of her head.

"One night this little piece of fluff walked into Emergency with a broken fingernail. Jeff went kind of goo-goo, and six months later he was married."

"Oh, Char."

"Story of my life," she said. "Men don't see me as the stuff of their romantic dreams. Their buddy, their colleague, yes. But girlfriend, lover, wife..." She shook her head.

"Well, they do now!"

"And look where that got me!"

"Yes! Smack dab in the middle of a romance. Okay, maybe not your first, though I personally think the Jeff thing doesn't even qualify. Lunch in the cafeteria. Ye gods, I know twelve-year-old teenyboppers who have a better feel for romantic ambience."

"It hurt. Isn't that a good enough qualification?"

Some of that hurt must have crept into her voice, because Mandy gave her a look loaded with sympathy.

"Have you been on the run ever since then, Char? Avoiding men?"

"I don't have time. And the heartache hurt my concentration."

"You're a woman ripe for romance. I'm really glad the mysterious Matthew Blake is here this summer."

"That's not a romance. How could it be? It's already over."

"Ha!"

"It is."

"I don't think so. In fact, if you'd care to make a small wager..."

"No, thank you." One thing she had learned was, never take a bet with Mandy. Her cousin was capable of moving heaven and earth to win.

"Just a small one. For your red belt."

"It would clash with your hair."

"Only if I wore it on my head."

"Mandy, if I took this bet, you might feel driven to play Cupid."

"You don't think I'd go to that length for a belt, do you?" Mandy asked innocently.

"Yes!" Charity said, without hesitation.

"By the way, what did Nelson get in return for taking your shift for you?"

"A dinner date."

Mandy laughed. "My goodness, this is turning into the summer of your dreams, isn't it?"

"You mean the summer of your dreams for me," Charity said, climbing into bed.

"Make sure and have dinner here. It'll make Matthew really jealous."

"I can't play games like that. Besides, I don't think he has those kind of feelings for me."

"You could find out a whole lot more about his feelings if you had dinner here—at the same time he has dinner. I think that's about seven every night."

"It would be shameless to use Nelson like that," Charity protested, but her indignation was mild. There was no sense in getting too worked up about Mandy.

Mandy reached out and turned off the light, and Charity felt grateful for the blessed darkness. This was the part that hurt, after all. The fact that he'd made love to her and then tried to brush her off. The fact that she didn't know what he was really feeling—and then she had closed the door on ever finding out.

Had she been premature? No. She remembered Jeff and the deep affection and caring she had felt for him. Mandy seemed to think you could have a summer of lighthearted fun without paying the price. And maybe if you were Mandy you could. But she wasn't interested in taking that kind of chance with her own heart. Not now. Not when her career was going to take so much of her energy and commitment in the next few years.

Maybe after that there would be time . . . for men, for romance . . . for a family . . . and babies.

She pressed the flat surface of her stomach, and felt a sudden shaft of pure fear.

No birth control. Great play, Dr. Marlowe, she berated herself. And then she sighed. Maybe Mandy was right. What happened happened; destiny was not to be thwarted by mere human ambition.

Finally, having tossed and turned forever, she went to sleep.

She braced herself to see Matthew the following day, but she didn't. She worried a bit if he had got back safely, but not enough to ask anyone if he had. Lord forbid that she should look interested in him. It had been bad enough that he thought she was interested before this had happened. It would be worse now.

Another day passed and then another. She did some of the things she had wanted to do. She suntanned and swam. She went for long solitary hikes along well-marked trails. She tried to think of nothing at all, but found her mind drifting back to that one subject all the time.

Had he left the resort? Surely she would have bumped into him by now... unless he was avoiding her.

Pretending to be on a stroll, she hiked up to the parking lot. The Mercedes was still there. He had got back that night, hadn't he? Were there bears in these woods? Maybe he'd been mauled. Maybe he was out there alone, needing help... Her thinking grabbed her and she raced down to the beach, and followed the rocky shoreline looking for signs of him, but saw nothing. No torn clothing caught on branches, no moans of pain emitting from the dark woods. She knew her imagination was going wild, and forced herself to stop and think.

She could follow the shoreline all the way to where they had pulled up that afternoon looking for shelter, but that would take hours. It would be much simpler to...

She swallowed her pride and sought out her cousin, who, naturally, knew everything about everybody at the resort.

"Mandy, have you seen Matthew?"

"Does this mean you are relenting on your original position?" Mandy asked hopefully.

"It means no such thing! I just haven't seen him since . . . you know . . . and I started to wonder if he even got back."

"He got back. In fact, I just saw him in the flesh, bruised as that might be."

"Bruised?" Charity asked weakly.

"It looks as if he must have had a run-in with a few trees finding his way home that night. Serves him right." Mandy took a look at Charity and hastened to assure her. "Superficial. A scratch on his nose. It's nothing. But you know where I saw him? In with Mrs. Foster. And she looked upset. I wondered right away if he'd registered a complaint against you, Charity. It doesn't look good dumping guests in the middle of the uncharted wilderness."

"I wouldn't exactly call it the uncharted wilderness."

"I don't think it matters what *you* call it. It matters what he calls it, if that's even what he's discussing. Honestly, he looked like an absolute bear. When I asked him about his nose he actually *growled* at me. Those bad-tempered brutes are so intriguing, aren't they?"

"Mandy, I might lose my job, and you're contemplating the intrigue of bad-tempered men."

"You won't lose your job. Mrs. Foster is too much of a softie to fire anyone. At most, she'll reprimand you, and she'd hate that so much she'd probably ask me to do it for her."

Just then, Donna, who worked on the front desk, came trotting across the lawn toward them.

"I've been looking for you two. Mandy, Mrs. Foster has called a staff meeting. What do you suppose that means?"

Mandy frowned. "I don't know. We've never had one before, have we?"

"Not that I can remember," Donna said glumly. "It's that man, I just know it."

"What man?" Mandy asked.

"Matthew Blake. He's been with her for three days now. They've been having their meals in her office. That's too much for an old lady."

Mandy shot Charity a wicked look. "Now that is one *long* complaint. Are you sure you told me everything about that night?"

Charity glared at her cousin, but Donna seemed too upset to notice. "Henri says he thinks he's from a big hotel chain, and he's trying to buy out Anpetuwi. Wouldn't that be awful?"

"Henri should stick to making soup," Mandy said, obviously not liking her position as first with the news being usurped. "I heard the Mafia loaned Mrs. Foster some money and he was sent to collect."

Donna gasped and looked at her, round-eyed. "Mandy, that's awful."

"Just have a look at him, the next time you go by. All that curly dark hair. When's this meeting, anyway?"

"Tomorrow at ten. Everybody has to be there. *Everybody.*" Donna scurried away to spread the news.

"Mandy, you really shouldn't have said that about the Mafia."

"Oh, why not? If we're going to have some rumors flying around they might as well be exciting ones. Now, I'm going to find out what's really going on."

But she didn't find out anything. And the next morning when she and Charity arrived at the meeting they were as much in the dark as everyone else.

The first person Charity saw was him. The meeting was being held in the dining room, and he was leaning his haunches against a table at the very front of the room, looking extremely cool and self-possessed. Her heart lurched.

He turned and looked at her, the welt across his nose red and ugly. His eyes narrowed on her, briefly, and then he picked up a file on the table beside him, and leafed through it, dismissing her.

She shrank into a seat near the back, her heart beating a mile a minute.

Well, she had wanted him to be hopping mad the next time she saw him, and she was pretty sure she'd succeeded.

The staff drifted in slowly, and finally at around ten-thirty everyone was accounted for.

Mrs. Foster was fluttering around like a nervous bird.

"Thank you all for coming," she finally said. "I think we can begin."

"I should certainly hope so," said Matthew. His tone gentled as he looked at Mrs. Foster. "Grandma, sit down. I'll look after it."

Grandma? Charity and Mandy exchanged surprised looks.

"All right, Matthew," Mrs. Foster said, wringing her hands, "but don't lose your temper. I hate it when you lose your temper."

A ripple of laughter went through the staff, but it was silenced instantly with a look from him.

"My grandmother is worried about heads rolling," he said quietly. You could have heard a pin drop. "I don't know why she would be concerned about that. Do any of you? It couldn't be because golf carts—" he leveled a look at Nelson "—are careening around the grounds with a complete lack of any regard for safety. Certainly it wouldn't be because staff sit around the lounge at night and make guests the butt of practical jokes." His eyes found Mandy and Charity, and he continued softly. "It wouldn't be because guests are being gossiped about, and even *spied* on through binoculars, would it?"

A few of the staff members exchanged uneasy glances. Most of them were looking studiously at their feet.

"This lodge has been in my family for three generations," Matthew continued. "It was the start of the F and B hotel chain, which I head. Anpetuwi has a reputation as one of the most renowned resorts in the world. But I have never seen such a total lack of staff discipline in my entire career in the hotel business.

"I appreciate that most of you love this place. I appreciate your fierce loyalty to it. I appreciate that many things are being done extremely well here. But I don't appreciate the fact that staff enjoyment seems to come ahead of enjoyment by the guests. I don't appreciate the fact that my grandmother has been taken advantage of."

This brought a collective gasp of protest.

"Now, Matthew, they just thought they were helping."

"As far as I can see," he continued, giving his grandmother a look of clearly mingled liking and exasperation, "my grandmother hasn't looked at an employment application in five years. Who the heck is doing the hiring and firing around here, anyway?"

"If you do a good job of hiring, nobody gets fired," Mandy muttered under her breath.

Charity shot her a shocked look, but Mandy was looking placidly ahead.

"There are going to be some changes in the next few weeks. I will be speaking to you each individually about your role in the future of the lodge. I will be running a tighter ship, and I will be speaking to each of you personally about my expectations of you.

"And if I could make one more suggestion—if I ask to see you at ten in the morning, and you wander in at ten-thirty, you will be looking elsewhere for employment. That will be all for today. If you will see Donna on your way out, she will let you know when your appointments are."

There was a general run for the door.

His voice stopped the stampede. "Miss Marlowe, I'll see you first. Right now, in the office."

Charity and Mandy both froze.

"Mandy," he clarified, though his eyes rested grimly on Charity.

She held his look, her head high, for as long as she could—all of about five seconds. Then she gave Mandy's arm a reassuring squeeze and followed the other employees out of the door.

She waited for Mandy in the main foyer. The minutes ticked by into an hour, and finally Mandy, looking only marginally subdued, came out of the office.

"Well?" Charity breathed, following her cousin out of the door.

"He confiscated my binoculars!" Mandy announced with mock outrage. "He said I have to balance my enthusiasm with maturity." She wrinkled her nose. "He said I don't always recognize the boundaries between having fun and being intrusive."

"Oh, Mandy."

"He said I don't always recognize the difference between being friendly and being familiar. Familiar. Isn't that a stuffy expression?"

"Oh, dear," Charity said with soft sympathy.

"But he also said he really admired my energy and loyalty to the lodge. He said he thought I had developed a very strong activity program, and that my rapport with the guests was incredible. He thanked me for helping take care of his grandmother."

"Speaking of that," Charity said cautiously, "you haven't been hiring people, have you?"

"Not exactly," Mandy said evasively. "I just could tell it was all getting to be too much for Mrs. Foster, and I've made some suggestions. She seemed relieved. I didn't tell him that, though. I still have a job, and I'd like to keep it that way. I really do love this old place."

"Were your feelings hurt by his criticism?"

"Strangely enough, no. I knew things were getting a little out of hand. I mean, we all have fun, and that's good, but there was nobody to say 'no,' when it needed to be said. That's not my strong suit, and it certainly isn't Mrs. Foster's. I'm glad he's here. It felt like a ship with no captain. Speaking of which, when do *you* see the captain?"

Captain Hook, she thought to herself. "Tomorrow, at four. I think I'm the last person he's seeing."

"Are you scared?"

"Yes."

SHE DID HER BEST to quell her inner quaking, but it couldn't have worked.

Matthew was sitting behind a big desk when she entered the office. He studied her thoughtfully, and then said softly, "You look nervous, Miss Marlowe."

"Do I?" She couldn't take her eyes off the livid scratch on his nose. It made him look more like a ruthless pirate than ever.

"Hmm." He came out from behind the desk, and gestured at the sofa. "Have a seat, won't you?"

She sat, trying to look everywhere but the deep-ocean blue of those eyes. The silence stretched. Finally, she looked at him.

"So where should we start?" he asked evenly. "With the other night? With my walk home? With your performance as a waitress? With your application form?"

"My what?" she squeaked.

He sat down beside her. She could smell the soap scent on his skin, a trace of after-shave, and an unidentifiable aroma of pure masculinity. He was so close that she could have touched him, and she wanted to touch him.

She pressed herself into her corner of the sofa.

"Okay. We'll start there." He shoved a paper at her. "Do you recognize this?"

What she recognized was Mandy's handwriting—big and round. Her name in Mandy's handwriting. Her eyes widened. Her name and much more. All her experience as a waitress. According to this, she was a student—the only part of the whole application, aside from her name, that had any truth to it. Mandy had shaved several years from her life, and put that she'd spent her last few summers working as a waitress at the Banff Springs Hotel. Charity nearly choked when she saw the title Other Interests. Under it Mandy had written, boldly, a single word: Men.

"Oh, Lord," Charity said, closing her eyes.

She opened them again to peek briefly at the signature. Something Marlowe. It could have been Charity, though it looked suspiciously like "Charlie," which was the name of Mandy's budgie.

She forced herself to meet his gaze. His expression was bland, and he obviously had no intention of filling the damning silence.

I really do love this old place, Mandy had said. Mandy, who had blacked Tommy Bellinger's eye because he had called Charity a four-eyed freak.

This application was wrong, but somehow it felt as if it would be a lot more wrong to turn Mandy in.

"I'm sorry," she said.

"So, this is basically a work of fiction." Matthew tapped the application. It placed his lean, tanned hand too close to hers. She stared at it, remembering.

"You as much as told me, the other night, that you didn't have any experience." She was fascinated by the brick red crawling up his neck. "As a waitress," he amended hastily.

"Yes," she said quietly, and with a certain dignity. "That application is a complete work of fiction."

"It's a very serious thing to lie on an application form."

"I realize that," she said.

"Then why?" The disappointment and the puzzlement in his eyes were slaying her, like a red-hot sword piercing her breast.

"I don't know," she said lamely.

"That's not good enough."

"I'll leave as soon as you can find a replacement," she said softly, looking at her shoes. "Sooner, if you'd rather."

"It's a little more complicated than that, isn't it?"

Her head shot up, and she stared at him. "I hope you don't think I would use what happened the other night in any way to try and influence you. What do you think I am?"

His gaze went from her face to the forged application form, then back to her face.

"I don't have a clue," he said softly. "A wildcat, and a virgin. A liar, and a saint. Incredibly soft. And ice hard."

"I'm not hard," she protested. Or a wildcat either, though she thought she'd better leave that one alone.

"That was a hard woman who laughed and left me stranded."

More like an actress lifted to greatness by pure desperation. "I'm sorry about that, too."

"Quit saying you're sorry!"

"Well, I am."

"I know you are! Don't you think I can *see?* Feel? What's real and what isn't?" His voice softened. "Sometimes I feel, when I look into your eyes, that I know you, right to your soul. And then—" he ran a harsh finger along the gash in his nose, and gestured impatiently at the paper in her hand "—the rug gets pulled out from underneath me."

"I said I'd leave."

"I don't want you to leave, damn it!"

It was there in the air between them, the attraction, the chemistry that smoked and bubbled deep within them, waiting, waiting, waiting...

"It would probably be better."

"It probably would," he snapped. "Do you understand now, why I said it was so wrong? I'm your boss. That kind of behavior is unacceptable between an employer and employee."

She felt herself flinch. For her it had been a night of mystery and of magic, and he had reduced it to "unacceptable behavior." Still, she sensed his deep self-censure.

"It's not as if you planned it," she said quietly, for some incomprehensible reason trying to ease his distress.

"I didn't plan it?" He laughed harshly. "Maybe I didn't. But I didn't think of anything else since the first moment I laid eyes on you, either."

She gasped at this admission, then realized he was just looking for ways to beat himself up. The first time he'd seen her, after all, she'd had her head wrapped in a towel. Hardly the stuff to fuel lustful fantasies!

"I'm giving us each a chance," he said coldly, getting up. "I'm giving myself a chance to behave like a decent guy, and you a chance to try being a waitress, since for some unfathomable reason it meant enough to you to lie to get the job. We've both made mistakes. Let's see if we can overcome them."

His back was to her. She could tell there was some great strain in him, just from the way he held himself.

She got up and slipped quietly out of the door.

The thunderheads were moving faster now, rolling right over her head, rumbling with dark warning.

She knew the right thing to do would be to leave, and the sooner the better. But she couldn't. And it wasn't out of her desire to be a waitress for the summer, either.

There was electricity in this air. Dangerous. Hot. Compelling. Addictive, somehow. She was caught in the seducing current, and she could not break free. And didn't want to.

CHAPTER SIX

"MANDY, YOU SAID the wind never blew here." Charity was slightly hunched over, holding down her skirt, a wide light blue denim.

"You're talking to me!" Mandy crowed.

"It's because we're about to declare a state of emergency," Charity responded dryly.

A gust of wind howled through the patio, lifted the edge of a tablecloth and dumped the contents of the drink-laden table on the floor. There were a few startled shrieks, but for the most part the patrons seemed to be enjoying the sudden element of adventure that had been added to their evening.

It wasn't that she hadn't been talking to Mandy, it was just that she had let her displeasure over that application be felt for an entire week now.

"I just filled the silly thing out so there would be something in the files, and they could prove employment in case an auditor ever came in," Mandy had said petulantly. "How was I supposed to know anybody would ever read the thing?

"Is all forgiven?" Mandy asked now, hopefully.

"Oh, I suppose," Charity said gruffly.

"You wouldn't believe how sexy that skirt is blowing around like that," Mandy said mischievously, now that she'd been granted her pardon. "Oh, thank God. There's Matthew."

Though she never thought she'd see the day when she'd be thankful for Matthew's presence in the same room as her, Charity silently echoed Mandy's gratitude, and held down her skirt even harder.

She watched as he quickly sized up the situation and then took command.

"Ladies and gentlemen," he called over the force of the wind, "would you please pick up your drinks and move inside?"

With her skirt billowing around her, Charity rushed out to grab empties off the tables before the wind shattered more of them.

"Mandy, Nelson," Matthew called, "the canoes need to be pulled up higher. Joe, our patrons are milling about in the dining room. Lock up here, but take a bottle of good brandy with you. Give each of our customers a free drink and then send them home."

"Yes, sir."

He was a whiz at this business, Charity thought with reluctant admiration. In the week that he'd been at the helm of the Anpetuwi ship there had been a remarkable change in atmosphere. It was running like a well-oiled machine, instead of like a slightly out-of-control summer camp.

And the funny thing was, instead of being resentful of the changes, everybody seemed happier, seemed to have more sense of purpose, more enthusiasm for giving the guests a good time, instead of having one themselves.

Matthew picked up a plastic tub and began to clear glassware from tables. That was another thing she'd noticed. He was a very hands-on kind of man. He seemed to know how to do everything that came with running a resort and he didn't seem to mind doing any of it. No wonder the staff respected him, and the guests liked him.

Still, she didn't think she could ever be comfortable with him, not after what had happened between them.

"Mr. Blake," she called, "I'm sure you're needed elsewhere—" but even before she could finish speaking another glass crashed off a table, and Charity, still doing battle with her skirt, went to pick up the fragments.

"Don't try to pick that up with your hands." Suddenly he was right beside her, her hand arrested in his own. She straightened and looked up at him, at the wind in his hair. He dropped her hand, but he didn't move.

"We'll leave the breakage until we can get a broom." His eyes narrowed on her wind-tossed hair and strayed down to the skirt that kept billowing up around her legs. He lifted a hand, and looked as if he was going to touch her cheek, and then dropped it.

"The storm flatters you, Miss Marlowe," he said gruffly.

She could have told him it did the same for him, but she didn't. "I'm sure I can manage without you." She whirled away from him, and began to take tablecloths off empty tables. She noticed that he continued to work, apparently unaware that he was entirely unsuited to be a gofer, and stifled a sigh.

She flounced past him, her arms full of table coverings. She tried to open the door to the storage room, but twice the wind blew it out of her hands. The third time the clasp jammed. Matthew came by her, and held open the door to the small room with a mawkish bow. She pretended not to see the light in his eyes; she pretended it was the wind going up her skirt that made her suddenly shiver with apprehension.

He neatly propped a chair in front of the door and went back about his business, but awareness of him tingled all around Charity—awareness of the way he moved, with such effortless grace, of the way he looked with the wind ravaging his neat curls.

A crash of thunder boomed so loudly that the floor shook. Charity felt a tickle on the back of her neck as lightning split the air. Her whole body tingled, as though somehow this was a moment it had anticipated, and been waiting for.

Nonsense, she told herself. The storm was just triggering memories of the last time they had been in a storm together. This was nothing the same.

Rain began to blow into the patio.

"Charity, give me a hand. We'll try and move some of the band's equipment into the linen closet so it doesn't blow over or get wet."

The equipment was usually quite well protected, but the wind was driving rain in where it usually did not reach.

She went over to him, and together they lifted a speaker.

"Is it too heavy?" His shirt was getting wet and moulding to the hard, enticing lines of his chest. The muscles in his arms bunched as he heaved the speaker up. She nearly gasped with dismay at the shock that shivered down into her tummy.

"Are you sure you're okay?"

"Fine," she said through clenched teeth.

They wrestled the speaker into the storage cupboard.

"Okay, set it down. Easy. Easy."

Bang.

They were instantly enveloped in total darkness. For a moment, she thought the lights had gone, but then she remembered that the Susweca was unencumbered by the modern convenience of electrical lights. The wind had once again slammed the door shut.

A few silent seconds ticked by. She could hear Matthew wiggling the door handle. She was even more aware of him in the total blackness than she had been before.

"Open the door!"

"I'm trying," he snapped.

"What do you mean, trying?"

Silence.

"Matthew?"

"The bloody thing seems to be locked."

"That's impossible." But with a sinking heart she remembered the sturdy latch jamming on her just moments ago.

She heard his sigh of impatience, and squeezed past the speaker, groping her way through the darkness to his side. She reached out, ran her hands down the door until she found the handle and twisted it.

Nothing. She jiggled it. Nothing. Her shoulder was brushing his arm, and she yanked on the door with strength born of pure panic.

"I hope you're not afraid of the dark," he commented, his tone dry and faintly sarcastic.

I'm afraid of you, she would have liked to scream, I'm afraid of you and me, and the things I feel when we're too close together.

"I'm not afraid of the dark," she said, "But I'm certainly not going to resign myself to spending the night in here."

"Oh? What are you going to do?"

Her eyes were adjusting to the darkness, and now she could see that he had folded his arms over the enticing broadness of his chest and was watching her with a challenging glitter in his eyes.

"Have you got a credit card?"

"That is a question every man dreads hearing from a pretty woman."

"This is no time for jokes!"

"It seems to me like the perfect time for a little humor."

She felt him press cold plastic into her hand, but she also felt the tingle of warmth from his fingers.

The sensation of desperation grew and clawed at her throat.

"So, what do you do with that thing now that you've got it?" he asked.

She was sure she could hear mocking in his tone. She forced her breathing to steady. If he could treat this lightly, so could she!

"I head for the nearest jewelry store," she said lightly, "which gives me all the more incentive to get this door open."

His teeth flashed briefly and brilliantly. "I think you've been watching too many movies."

She turned hastily from the light of that smile and slid the credit card into the crack between the door and the frame. She forced it up and down, just as they seemed to do in the movies.

"Ouch," she yelped.

"What?"

"I broke a fingernail."

"So much for a career as a burglar, though I can understand why it might appeal."

"Why?"

"No application forms. Here. Give me that thing. I'll try it."

Their hands brushed again in the darkness. Her comeback to the application dig died in her throat. His hand touching hers in the absolute darkness, his fingertips lingering on her fingertips just a moment longer than was necessary, was just about the most sensual feeling she had ever had.

Of course, she reminded herself sternly, that was just proof that she had not had many sensual encounters. Nevertheless, she tucked her hands safely into the pockets of her big skirt. She noticed how damp it was, and tried not to shiver.

"It doesn't work," he finally said. "I guess my credit rating is safe for the time being."

The room was so tiny. He seemed to fill it—the very air she was breathing seemed to be full of him, air that he had pulled deep into his lungs first...

"You could break the door down!"

"I suppose I could try." He sounded decidedly unenthusiastic. "They built things differently back in the old days. That door is more likely to break my shoulder than my shoulder break the door."

"You don't look like a wimp," she taunted. The taunt was a measure of her pure and desperate need to get out of this very small room with this very attractive man.

It seemed the aroma of him was growing all around her, damp and masculine, the smell of rain in a forest.

"I could make you take that back," he said, his voice a low growl very close to her ear. His breath fanned across her neck and raised goose bumps on it.

"I'm sorry," she said faintly. "I just don't like being...trapped." He was so close she could feel the heat coming off his body.

"Claustrophobic?" he asked. He moved a step away from her. There seemed to be genuine concern in the question.

If it was claustrophobia this was its first appearance in her life. No, this phobia seemed to relate directly to Matthew Blake. To close encounters with Matthew Blake.

"No, not claustrophobia, just—" Her voice faded. Just what, after all? Fear of a good-looking man? Fear of chemistry? Fear of herself?

"Well, I'll give it a try. Stand back. There's no sense both of us getting knocked silly."

Obediently, she squeezed herself against a shelf.

She saw the shadow of him move back and then charge toward the door.

"Umph!" He bounced off it, and landed on the floor. "Dammit! Did that ever hurt." He cursed, and then fell silent. She was fighting with herself about whether to draw nearer to him, despite the danger of that, and see if he was all right, when he spoke again. "This is the age of equal rights. Why the hell didn't you throw yourself at the door?"

She didn't exactly throw herself against the door, but she began to beat on it with her fists. "Help," she shouted. "Help. Let us out of here!"

"Miss Marlowe?"

"What?"

"I am going to have ruptured eardrums to go along with my mangled shoulder."

His voice was soft as the black velvet darkness in the room.

"I want out of here," she said, "and I want out of here now."

"Are you about to panic?" he asked softly. He got up, and loomed out of the darkness. A hand settled on her shoulder. She could feel the iron strength in it. And the warmth. She could feel her skin tingling with delighted response. Yes, she was about to panic!

She took a deep breath. Of course she wouldn't panic. Doctors did not panic. His hand was still on her shoulder; a finger touched her neck, tickled there.

"I want out of here," she said again.

"I do, too," he said, his voice low and reassuring, the voice one might use on a frightened child. "And we'll be out of here soon. Joe will come back to lock up—"

"He already locked up!"

"Or Mandy will come looking for you."

Mandy would remember exactly whom she had left her cousin with, and when Charity didn't appear at their cabin she would probably chortle with devilish delight, roll over and go to sleep.

"We could be in here twenty-four hours," she whispered.

"Not likely," he said, his voice still soft and calm. "But we might as well try and get comfortable, hmm?"

She was reacting to the soft note in his voice, letting it wash over her and slow down the beat of her heart.

"What are you doing?" she asked, her heart picking up the pace again.

"I'm taking off my shirt."

She flattened herself against the door. Sure enough, her eyes could see the faint satiny gleam of his bronze skin. The white of his shirt floated, ghostlike, to the floor.

"Why?" she squeaked.

"It's wet. I'm cold. Maybe you should do the same thing."

"Are you crazy?"

"Look, Charity, let's get it out in the open, okay?"

She said nothing.

"This is an awkward situation. It's uncomfortable. Maybe it's even dangerous, but it won't make it any more comfortable, or safe, to be huddled around in wet clothes. I'm going to wrap up in one of the linens. I suggest you do the same."

"I'm not cold. And I'm certainly not taking off my clothes." The unspoken "again" sizzled in the air between them.

"Your teeth are chattering," he said dryly. He passed her something warm and dry—a tablecloth, she guessed. She pressed it against herself, squinting at him through the darkness.

"Just wrap up in it, toga-style."

"Toga?" she squeaked.

"An unfortunate choice of phrase," he admitted. "Charity, I'm going to turn around. I can't see you very well anyway, but I'm going to turn around, and count to two hundred. Slowly. If you aren't out of those wet clothes by then, I'll get you out of them myself."

"How dare you?"

"How dare you prevent me from making myself really sick, Matthew?" he taunted. "I think I'll sue you."

He was right, and she knew it. The linen area was unheated, and though they were well protected from the ravages of the wind she was aware of her damp clothing chilling her skin, the rough chattering of her teeth. But, given her and Matthew's history, maybe a chill was less danger than being naked under a tablecloth in this small room with him.

"Fifty," he informed her cheerfully.

He wouldn't really strip the wet clothing from her himself...would he? It would be dangerous enough with some space and several tablecloths between their nearly naked bodies, but if he touched her she knew she would be lost.

"Seventy-five."

"Okay, okay," she snapped. Hurriedly, she peeled the damp clothes from her chilled skin. She stepped out of them quickly, and wrapped a tablecloth securely around her. It did feel wonderful. For added warmth, and a touch more security, she grabbed another one and wrapped that one around herself, too. She felt far more...dressed...than she had thought she would.

"Two hundred. Are you finished?"

"Yes."

He turned back toward her. Even in the darkness she caught the sweep of his eyes touching her naked shoulders. But his voice was all business. "Okay. Now I'm going to pull down a whole pile of these things and make a nest out of them so we'll be warm and cozy until we're rescued from each other."

So he, too, realized that the real trap was not the locked door. Was he, too, remembering the last time they had decided to keep each other warm?

She squinted through the darkness at him, wishing it were dark enough to hide the hard gleam of his muscles, the masculine perfection of him. But it wasn't. If anything, watching bits and pieces of his perfectly chiseled anatomy appear out of the murky darkness, and then disappear again, was an experience that was faintly and uncomfortably erotic. She ordered herself to stop looking at him, but there seemed nowhere else to look, and somehow her greedy eyes would not shut.

"Charity, come over here."

No, a self-protective voice inside her answered, but it never made it outside her. After all, it was join him or prop up the door for a few hours. Twenty-four hours, the way her luck ran when it concerned this man.

"I'm going to feel like an idiot if someone comes and opens that door right now," she muttered, using words like a shield to try and hide her real distress, the real reason she was feeling like an idiot. A breathless, wonder-struck idiot.

"I don't think you're in much danger."

That showed what he knew.

Carefully, she made her way to where he had laid a pile of tablecloths on the floor. She sank down, as far away from him as was humanly possible, which wasn't very far. The bed he had made was small. And cozy. That broad and naked shoulder was only inches from her.

"Relax," he said. "The tension is coming off you like little arrows."

Ridiculously, a song that had been popular in her childhood flooded her mind. She laughed nervously.

"Share the joke?"

She did, and she could see his white smile, brilliant, in the blackness of the room.

"I remember that song." He sang a few bars of it in a lusty baritone that filled the darkness, and oddly enough dispelled some of the tension that had been growing in her. "Sing," he commanded.

She wasn't good at being silly, but she gave herself over to the moment. If you couldn't fight it, why not join it? Here she was, locked in a cupboard, and wrapped in a tablecloth. Why not give herself over to the silliness of it, instead of feeling distress?

They sang every song they knew, which between them did not add up to very many songs. But it did break down some of the unbearable tension that had been building. It shut out the noise of the storm—

Until the sound of their voices, and their laughter, died, and in their place was an even more acute awareness than there had been before.

They had just played together. And laughed together. It had been a mistake.

His hand touched hers.

She pulled away, but his hand followed, and took hers in an unrelenting grasp.

"I just want to show you something."

He took her protesting hand, and laid it on a thick roll of tablecloths between their bodies. She had been so busy avoiding touching him, she had not even noticed it was there.

"What's that supposed to be?"

"A bolster. Does that make you feel safer?"

Oh, sure, about as safe as a shield of plastic wrap would make her feel if a bear were charging toward her at a full gallop.

"Is it a joke?" she said nervously. "Or is it supposed to do something?"

"I'm going to lie down and go to sleep now. And it's supposed to keep me from reaching out for you in the night, wrapping my arms around you, letting my lips tangle in your hair..."

"Okay. I get the point." She sat stiffly, aware of him nestling down beside her, yearning for his arms to wrap around her and his lips to tangle in her hair.

"Aren't you going to lie down?"

"I'm not tired."

"You're not tired, or you don't want to let your defenses down?"

She didn't answer, though she silently cursed his astuteness.

The silence crept around them, as thick as the darkness. Charity listened, straining her ears for the sound of someone coming.

"What are you a student in, Charity?"

"Sciences," she said abruptly. That damn application. Would it haunt her all the days of her life?

"Sciences," he said thoughtfully. "I would never have guessed it, but I like it. Strangely, I can picture you in a white jacket dismembering rats."

"I hope you're being sarcastic—as usual."

"All right. I'll take back the part about the rats."

"That leaves the white jacket. And the context that most people put white jackets into is hardly flattering."

He laughed, a low rumble, not so unlike the thunder that was unrelentingly outside the door.

"You don't want me to start flattering you," he said dangerously.

"No! But I don't want to be seen as a candidate for a straitjacket, either. It makes for poor tips."

"Pardon me. Of course, I don't think you're crazy. A scientist who wants to be a waitress for the summer. That's pretty normal stuff."

"I didn't say I was a scientist," she said grumpily.

"Hmm. Sciences. Biology. Chemistry. Physics. That's it! A rocket designer. NASA's most glamorous Space Shuttle programmer...who does a little waitress work on the side."

"I'm not a Space Shuttle programmer—"

"Right. You would have made short work of the lock if you were inclined that way."

"And I'm not glamorous, and I don't have any ambition to be either one."

"You're pushing me in the direction of flattery again," he said softly. "There's no telling where that might go."

"I was not fishing for compliments!"

"When a beautiful woman denies she's beautiful, she's hinting."

"Well, I wasn't. I don't even like the *word* glamorous—it's slick and artificial sounding."

"What was your minor in? Semantics?" His voice was full of dark humor, dark humor to match that dark hair, and the sun-darkened surface of his skin. Why could a man's voice in the night create an ache in a person so deep and so wide that it felt as if it could never be filled?

"Why don't you go to sleep?" she suggested with exasperation, though a little tiny part of her was rising to the verbal sparring with him, taking a perverse pleasure in the challenge of matching wits with him.

Things were going from bad to worse. He wasn't just attractive, damn him, he was also interesting.

"I'm not tired, either. What did you get for your tenth birthday?"

"What?" she asked, astonished.

"For your tenth birthday. It's just a game to pass some time away. We have quite a lot of it, I suspect."

For some reason it felt as though she was being sucked into something by a cardsharp. Attractive. Interesting. Fun. A woman had better keep her wits about her.

"My tenth birthday," she mulled over, warily. "I don't know. A chemistry set, I think."

"The little scientist even then!"

"I was considered an unusual child," she said slowly. Even now, she felt herself cringe at the way he'd said "little scientist," all those childhood hurts about being "different" flooding back. People had actually laughed at her for asking for a chemistry set instead of a Barbie doll or a set of Nancy Drew books.

"In what way?" he asked softly, his tone completely changed, as if he knew they had come to tread on sensitive ground.

"I was very smart." She said this stiffly, not wanting to be accused of bragging—something else that had happened to her when she was a child, and she just stated a fact, or answered a question.

"What did you get on your math test, Charity?" that horrible Tommy Bellinger had asked her. One hundred, she had said. "Bragger, bragger," he had shouted with horrendous hostility. The same scenario had played itself out in a hundred different ways when she was a child. "Quit using those big words to impress people," when she hadn't been aware she was using big words. "You're not really reading that book, you're just trying to look smart," when she sat under a tree with some well-worn treasure.

"Did you think I'd be surprised?" he asked gently.

"I can't even remember the price of a Canadian Club and Coke," she reminded him.

"All the really intelligent people I've met, and I mean that in a clinical sense, have a sort of specialized intelligence. They might be excellent at math—but they stumble over their tongues saying good morning to the mailman."

That was definitely her, she thought wryly.

"Though you're extremely articulate," he continued. "It's one of the things that didn't—doesn't—ring true about your current status as a cocktail waitress. But you aren't going to enlighten me, are you?"

"I'm just a broke student trying to earn some money over the summer, and I don't think I'm all that articulate." Especially around him. She didn't have a clue how to relate to men—or at least not in the way her peers, someone like Mandy, would.

"I'm sorry. That you were lonely as a child."

And she was sorry he'd said that. She was having enough trouble fending off his considerable charms. Attractive. Interesting. Fun. Compassionate. Sure. What was he, the perfect man? He'd loved her and left her once, and if she gave him a chance he'd do it again.

"What about you, Matthew Blake?" she asked lightly. "What did you get on your tenth birthday?"

"A dinghy to explore the lake. I grew up here, you know, at the lodge."

"Did you? It must have been a wonderful place to grow up."

"It was. My family's history is very tied to this lodge. My great-grandfather built the lodge. He was single at the time, but not for long. My great-grandmother's family were here the opening week."

"That's very romantic," Charity said.

"If you like romance, it gets better. Do you like romance, Charity?"

"Not generally," she said, her voice clipped.

Matthew laughed, a low laugh. "I'll tell you the rest of the story anyway. They got married here, on the very deck outside that door, actually. It wasn't a lounge then, just a big sundeck."

"That's where Mrs. Foster met her husband, too!" Charity remembered.

"That's right. She was their daughter. They had three of them. All of them met their husbands here at the lodge."

"My goodness, that's a coincidence." Charity was not sure why she suddenly felt so...uneasy was not quite the word. But not alone. This place had bred romance after romance, and it was as if it was that she had felt tingling in the air all night, like a presence...

"And then my mother met my father here."

Her mouth was getting dry.

"Really?"

"He was the Blake. He actually came representing the Blake hotel and resort chain. He was going to try for a buyout. Instead he fell in love with my mother. After their marriage they amalgamated the two operations, and formed the F and B chain. My father had always been fast-paced and high-powered, but he fell in love with this place. We could hardly get him away from here. But when my mother died he couldn't handle it here anymore. Too many memories, I suppose. We moved to London, as most of our resorts are in Great Britain. He became more active in the business again, and I grew up learning the ropes."

"So why did you come back?" she asked. She felt nervous of his reply. It seemed the family found husbands here, and brides. She felt almost dizzy thinking about it. About the life matches that had been brewed here, come to life under this moon, and these rough-hewn walls. Generation after generation.

"Gran needed help. She comes to London, too, for the off-season, and she's been fiercely proclaiming her ability to do things herself here, but..." He shook his head. "It's hard to see someone you love so much fading. I just didn't want her trying to run it by herself anymore. She feels her failure very sharply even though she won't admit it."

"She's a lovely woman."

"And a pushover."

"I don't feel anyone here has taken advantage of your grandmother, Matthew. If anything, they pulled together to try and protect her from those very failures you think hurt her so much."

He sighed. "I know that. I guess I know that. Some of the things that happened may have been misguided, that's all."

She realized they were back at her application form. But somehow she was unthreatened. The ghosts of love were all around her, holding her somehow. His grandparents had met here. And his parents. And he had met her here.

She knew it was foolish. She knew it didn't make one rational bit of sense. But suddenly all that rational thinking that she had been clinging to all night was gone, gone in a puff of smoke, gone in one long and loud roll of thunder.

"Matthew, I want you to hold me."

There was a long silence. "Do you know what you're asking?" he finally growled.

"Yes," she whispered. "I know exactly what I'm asking."

He lifted her easily over the bolster. His arms around her felt so right, like homecoming.

"Lord, Charity, it's what I want, too." His lips welcomed her, touching her nose and her cheeks and her eyes, wandering down her neck.

He rolled her over, patting her on the bottom, staring down at her, running his fingers through her hair.

"Charity, I said I wouldn't let this happen again. I promised myself."

She drew his head down to her mouth and engaged his lips in a tender argument.

"Charity! Matthew!"

They looked at each other for a long time. Heard the tapping of Mandy's heels grow close.

Time stood still, and for a suspended moment she hoped. But then Matthew put her gently away.

"We're in here," he called. His eyes rested on her face once more, with an expression so baffling that she could not hope to interpret it. "Mandy?" He rose, and walked over to the door, scooping up his shirt on the way. "We're in here."

"What? Oooh! I can't get the door open. It's jammed. I'll be right back with help."

Charity quickly got up, proudly dropped the tablecloths and got dressed. She made no attempt to hide herself, in some strange way, completely out of character for herself, taunting him with the choice he had made. And he made no attempt to turn away.

"Just for the record," he said softly, the desire burning hot in his eyes, "that was the hardest thing I've ever done."

She did turn from him then, to tuck her shirt in her waistband, and to hide the baffling tears that stung at her eyes.

They could hear Nelson and Joe working good-naturedly on the door, but not another word passed between them.

And when the door finally flew open it was Mandy who first saw them. Though they were standing as far apart as they could, and though they were both fully dressed, her hand flew to her mouth and her eyes widened.

"Oh, Lord," she said. Her eyes remained on Charity, though she addressed Matthew. "Mr. Blake, your fiancée just arrived from England."

CHAPTER SEVEN

CHARITY STIFLED her dismayed gasp, and then raised her head in public denial of the private humiliation that was curling in her belly like a coil of smoke. Though she wanted to run, she forced herself to walk, with what she could only hope was regal grace, past Matthew and out of the confines of that cupboard.

"I wish it had been me," Nelson said, grinning at her, oblivious to the undertows that swirled around him.

Matthew shot him a black look. Mandy elbowed him in the stomach. Charity kept walking.

Over her shoulder she could hear Joe. "Mr. Blake, we've got problems. A generator is down, and the wind took out several trees. The phone's out..."

She supposed some small part of her had hoped that he would come after her. But he didn't. It was Mandy who came alongside her.

"I'm sorry," Mandy murmured.

"About what?" Charity asked, with a great effort at surprise.

"That he has a fiancée."

"I couldn't care less—"

"Oh, don't put on the brave front for me! It's very obvious that the two of you did not pass the time playing tic-tac-toe."

"What do you mean, it's obvious we weren't playing tic-tac-toe?" Charity asked dangerously.

"The look on your face was like a naughty schoolgirl who'd just been caught with a stolen pie. And what on earth were you doing in that closet together in the first place?"

"We were moving the band's equipment out of the bad weather when the door blew shut and jammed."

Mandy looked incredulous, and then delighted. "Charity, if you can't see destiny at work in all this, you're blinder than your glasses, thick as they were, ever led me to believe."

"Let's just drop it," Charity suggested unhappily.

But Mandy wasn't prepared to drop it yet. "If it helps, his fiancée has not exactly endeared herself to anyone in the short time that she's been here. You should have heard her when nobody knew where Matthew was."

"It doesn't help. I don't want to hear about it." But a part of her did, and so she didn't stop Mandy as she continued to talk while they made their way up the hill toward their cabin.

"I was in the lobby when she came in. She was furious that she had to walk down the hill in her six-inch heels. She was wearing a dress that fitted like a snake's skin, and looked like one, too. Her hair, which is down to her bum, and a color of gold one only gets with a little help from Miss Clairol, was an absolute mess from the wind.

"Anyway, Donna was going crazy with the generator out and the phone down, and this princess says *loudly* she's Matthew Blake's fiancée and she wants a room, right now.

"Every room here has been booked since a year ago, and I was dearly hoping Donna would screw up the nerve to send her packing, but Mrs. Foster happened by, and Matthew's fiancée recognized her. She did this amazing transformation from a dragon to a buttercup, and within seconds Mrs. Foster offered to have her in her suite. I heard Mrs. Foster ask her if Matthew knew she was coming, and she said it was a surprise."

"Mandy, when are you going to stop eavesdropping?"

"I'll say it was a surprise," Mandy continued with grim satisfaction. "Did you notice Matthew's face when I said she was here? It got dark as thunder. He did not look very happy about the arrival of his fiancée."

They arrived at the cabin. It seemed cozy and welcoming, though suddenly red gingham—the same pattern as those tablecloths that had become beds and togas—did funny things in the region of her heart. Charity let Mandy chatter on and on, offering no comment, her feelings frozen somewhere deep within her. She knew Mandy wasn't normally catty, and that her comments about Matthew's fiancée were supposed to be making her, Charity, feel better.

As if anything could make her feel better. She had propositioned a man. In a moment of utter madness, she had offered herself shamelessly to Matthew. An *engaged* man.

Her heart had been on her sleeve when Mandy had opened that door, and she felt utterly and abjectly humiliated.

She took off her clothes. They still were faintly damp, and it felt good to be rid of them. Without even bothering to put on her pyjamas, she slid in between her sheets. She had never felt so exhausted. She closed her eyes and slept.

Bang. Bang. Bang.

Charity tried to prise her eyes open, but, failing that, she pulled her pillow over her head, and tried to ignore the noise outside. Somebody building something, she surmised sleepily; she had heard chainsaws going continuously almost from the moment she had gone to bed.

"Wake up, sleepyhead."

Her eyes flashed open. That deeply masculine voice, far too close to her ear, could only belong to one person. Cautiously she turned from the wall. She gasped and pulled her covers around her chin.

"Come on," he teased. "I've seen you in a toga."

"You have not," she said stiffly. "It was dark in there." She was very aware of her naked skin underneath those covers—which was ridiculous. She generally wasn't aware of her naked skin underneath the cover of her clothes.

"I have the night vision of a cat."

"To go with your morals," she muttered.

"I beg your pardon?"

She decided not to pursue this avenue of discussion, since, as she recalled the situation, it was not his morals but her own that had collapsed under the pressure of forced companionship with him.

"What are you doing here? This is my bedroom." She noticed suddenly how tired he looked; weariness had taken some of the sparkle from those blue eyes. His face was dark-shadowed with whisker growth. "Haven't you been to bed yet?"

Given the arrival of his fiancée, it occurred to her that the question was inappropriately personal. And even if it wasn't too personal, did she really want him to know that some wee devil of tenderness pulled at her heart at the gray lines of weariness etched into his face?

"I haven't been to bed yet," he said, not taking the question any way at all. "There was too much work to be done because of the windstorm. Some of it couldn't wait."

He sank down onto the edge of her bed, and she scurried over toward the wall, taking every inch of her covers with her.

He was dressed in a flannel shirt that was covered in sawdust. As soon as he had sat down beside her, the smell of him had enveloped her—man smells of sawdust, and soap, mingled with sweat. He seemed big and rugged—more like a logger than a hotel executive at this moment.

His eyes rested on her face with devastating scrutiny. "And I didn't feel this could wait, either. I wanted to talk to you."

"It could have waited," she said uneasily.

"I didn't think so."

"So you just barge into my bedroom and wake me up?"

"Mandy said it would be okay."

She closed her eyes in long suffering. Mandy. A little devil disguised as an elf.

"Mandy was wrong. I want you out of my room. I want you off my bed." I want you out of my life. "I'm tired. I want to go back to sleep."

"Tired?" He frowned. "You know it's nearly five o'clock in the afternoon, don't you?"

She felt a tiny shock. Five o'clock? She and Mandy had finally got in from last night's fiasco around four in the morning. She had slept thirteen hours? And still felt washed out and without energy? She was a person accustomed to getting seven hours of sleep, on a good night, and less most of the time.

Okay, so she wasn't going back to sleep. And he wasn't getting off her bed. "Spit it out, then," she said as ungraciously as she could.

"I just wanted you to know Sandra's not my fiancée."

Her heart did a ridiculous dance inside her chest. "Why should I care?"

"I wouldn't ever have—" He hesitated, struggling for words. "I wouldn't ever have been so intimate with you if I had had an obligation to someone else. At least, I hope I wouldn't have."

She stared at him. Those last words had come hard to him. His eyes were on her face. She dearly wished he would look at his toes, or out the window, or anywhere but into her eyes.

"I don't know, Charity. You pull me, like steel to a magnet. You make a little crazy. I've been a man in total control all my life, and I find myself out of control around you. I don't like that. I don't know how to fight it, either."

He was giving words to her own struggle, but before she could feel too much empathy a light went on inside her.

"You had a fight with her, didn't you? That's why you're here."

He smiled, a crooked smile that held no pleasure. "My broken engagement to Miss Sandra Bamfield is part of the reason I'm on this side of the ocean, I guess." Something darkened in his eyes.

What was it? she wondered sickly. Some passion he still held for his fiancée?

"Well, she's here, so she must think there is some chance of patching things up—not that it's any of my business, and not that I care."

He did a funny thing. He reached out and ran a hand through her hair. "You have makeup all over your face," he said. "And your hair is every which way. And you know something? You're still beautiful."

With a strange and tender little kiss on the tip of her nose, he departed.

She got up shortly after, and looked at herself in the mirror. If he thought that was beautiful he was not exactly the tasteful, classy guy he appeared to be, she thought, attempting to be callous.

But then Matthew was not what he appeared to be. And never had been. Underneath those precisely tailored silk shirts was a man so rugged and so real he could steal your breath away—if you let him.

And the trick was not to let him.

But somehow this latest encounter with Matthew had been even more disturbing than their encounter in the cupboard. She had to acknowledge that she was having extremely strong feelings for her enigmatic boss—feelings that were defying her ability to control them.

"Oh, come on," she muttered to herself. "You have more grit than that." And what she didn't have in grit she most certainly had in ethics. Matthew Blake was taken. Not officially, according to him, but she was certain his fiancée would tell a different story. She obviously would not have traveled such a huge distance if she did not hold out hope for the relationship, and Charity wanted to respect that. In fact, it gave her a perfect excuse to try, yet again, to get this wayward heart of hers under control.

Mandy bounced in the door. "They've had a furious fight already," she announced gleefully.

Charity, trying to repair her face, shot her a baleful look.

"Billie, the chambermaid, heard them this morning."

"I don't want to hear it. Mandy, this kind of gossip is intolerable." Of course, she really wanted to hear every detail. But she also wanted to get out of this mess with an ounce of pride, and she wasn't going to be able to do that if she was garnering details about Matthew from the chambermaids, even if it was through Mandy!

She picked up a brush and began to attack her hair. Matthew's assessment had been embarrassingly accurate.

"You're such a prude sometimes," Mandy said, but she said it with easy affection. "Anyway, they aren't really engaged. Don't you want to know that much?"

"Matthew already told me, thank you."

Mandy's eyes widened. "He did? That's what he wanted when he came up here? Goodness gracious, I thought he was changing your shift schedule! This is super!"

"It's no such thing."

"He practically told you he was available. Don't you find that exciting?"

"Not particularly, and I'll thank you in the future not to be telling men it's okay to come into my room. I didn't have a stitch on."

"I know," Mandy said fiendishly, "and I bet he knew, too!" At the look on Charity's face she added hastily, "For heaven's sake, you were under the blankets!"

"Mandy, absolutely no more meddling in my personal affairs. Is that clear?"

"Oh, all right," Mandy said, with insincere petulance. "Oh, by the way, I told Nelson tonight would be an excellent night for you two to go out for dinner together."

Mandy ducked, laughing, just as Charity's brush whizzed by her head.

"But it's your night off," she hooted, as she ran for the door. She popped her head back in, and widened her eyes innocently. "And I did arrange it *before* I promised to stop meddling."

"I am never speaking to you again," Charity threatened.

"That only lasted a week last time," Mandy taunted, with no concern at all. "Nelson will be here at seven. And, dearie, you'll need every minute of it. You are a mess."

"Thank you so much," Charity said grimly.

"You know something?" Matthew Blake had said. *"You're still beautiful."* It was disturbing, in an invigorating sort of way, because it had always been Mandy who saw her beauty, no matter what.

Of course, he was probably just a smoothie, so suave and slick that he could keep about three million women on the line at once.

Suddenly she was glad she was having dinner with Nelson. With any luck, it would take her mind off Matthew Blake.

Of course, she should have realized by now that luck did not run in her favor where Matthew was concerned.

Nelson had planned to take her to town, but when they got up to the parking lot he couldn't get his car to start.

He was so embarrassed, and she couldn't make the sting of it even worse by refusing when he suggested dining at the resort restaurant instead.

And, of course, Matthew was there. With the woman who could only be his fiancée.

Mandy had just left out one crucial detail when she described the young woman who had arrived from England.

She was beautiful. Extraordinarily, earth-stoppingly beautiful.

Bravely, Charity linked her arm through Nelson's as they were guided to a choice table overlooking the lake. To her credit, she tried very hard not to even once look over at the table, though she was being subjected to the constant tinkle of happy laughter, which made her think Matthew must be at his witty best.

Once, she did slide just the briefest look that way—to find Matthew, rather than being happily engrossed in entertaining his giggly companion, staring blackly right at her.

"So, what's your favorite TV show?" Nelson asked her.

"I don't have a TV," she said, doing her best to earn this very expensive dinner by giving him all her attention.

"No TV?" he asked. "What the heck do you do for fun?"

"Um—fun," she said, somewhat desperately. "Fun. I go for walks, sometimes, when I have time. I like books a lot." Nelson looked openly horrified. "I guess I haven't had much time for...fun."

"Oh, yeah. Mandy told me that. You're a student, huh?"

"Yes. And what about you, Nelson?"

She tried to get the focus off herself, but it became painfully obvious, very quickly, that she and Nelson had zilch in common. She felt awkward and inadequate. She felt that Nelson was bored and it was her fault. It was a familiar feeling. It reminded her of why she had started refusing most invitations to date a long time ago.

Dinner was exquisite, even though they ate it in the somewhat strained silence of two people who had discovered they had absolutely nothing to say to each other.

Her eyes strayed to Matthew's table. Why was it she'd never seemed to bore him? To have trouble talking to him? Or understanding him?

She noticed his fingers drumming on the table as his fiancée—ex-fiancée—chatted on and on. Was it possible that he felt bored? He suddenly looked up and caught her looking at him. He scowled.

She looked away.

"Do you want to go dancing?" Nelson asked.

It was the weekend, and the band would be in the Susweca.

She felt like an utter failure. "Nelson, I've just never been much of a dancer. I'm sorry."

"It's okay. But you know," he said wistfully, "you look different from how you are."

"You thought I was going to be a lot more fun, didn't you?" she asked gently.

He blushed.

"Nelson, I'm older than you, by quite a few years."

"Are you?" he said with relief, as if that explained everything. "You know, you're awfully smart, too. That kind of scares a guy, when you use big words like that."

He said this kindly, as if he meant it as a tip she could use on her next date—which obviously was not going to be with him.

She laughed, and he smiled. "I like you anyway," he assured her. "Like, you're the kind of person I'd like to talk to if I just had a fight with my girlfriend or was in trouble with the law or something."

She laughed again. Though most people would not have found it flattering, she did. She was not the kind of person who was fun, but she was the kind of person that people trusted, and that was a fair trade to her.

He walked her out the doors and down the steps, and kissed her on the cheek as if she were an old maiden aunt he had developed a polite affection for.

"See you around, eh?" And then he was off at his usual Nelson pace, shaking off sophistication eagerly.

She laughed as she watched him go.

"So was your evening delightful?"

She started, and then noticed the red glow of a cigarette tip in the night. Matthew was standing in the darkness underneath the eaves.

"It was... umm fun," she said out of some kind of loyalty to Nelson's masculine ego. She ordered herself to leave, to walk up to her cabin, but she stood rooted to the spot as he came down the stairs toward her.

"You didn't look as if you were having much fun," he said dangerously.

"In fact, neither did you," she shot back.

"Up to your old tricks, Charity? Are you still spying on me?"

"It's too bad you can't put your ego in a box, tie a rock to it and throw it out into the lake," she said sweetly. "*You* were the one who commented on my evening first."

"I was just teasing you. Has anyone ever told you you're very serious?"

"I have heard that once or twice," she admitted. She looked at him. Really looked. She had the oddest desire to touch the dark curls that danced on his head. She looked away. "When did you start smoking those filthy things again?"

"Very recently, actually," he said, flinging the cigarette away. "I've been finding life somewhat... frustrating." In his voice was a hint of dry self-mockery.

Charity was thankful for the cover of darkness. She hoped it hid from him the blush that fired her cheeks. She knew exactly the kind of frustration he was referring to... and exactly the closet it had come from!

"So tell me, in the closet with me one moment, out for dinner with another man the next. You must find the social whirl exhilarating.

"You needn't say I was in the closet with you in that tone of voice," she hissed at him.

"What tone?" he asked with counterfeit surprise.

"As if I were some lusty maid who waylaid you—"

He burst out laughing. "So which of us do you like better?" he asked silkily. "Nelson or me?"

"Don't be ridiculous. I don't like either of you, in that way. Nelson is a boy—"

"I'm glad you see that," he interjected quietly.

"And you are—" She faltered, searching for words.

"A man," he suggested softly.

"A boor," she suggested, with no softness at all.

He laughed again. "Maybe we should clarify what you mean by 'that way,'" he suggested, leaning toward her, the smoky smell of him oddly intoxicating.

"Darling!"

They snapped apart as though they were on a rubber band. "A boor who is spoken for," Charity reminded him in an undertone.

"There you are." The woman floated down the steps toward them on the cloud of her gossamer gown.

Matthew's face was impassive. "This is my friend, Sandra Bamfield," he said, with absolute decorum. "Charity Marlowe."

Charity was very aware of two things: that Matthew made no attempt to define his relationship with her, and that Sandra Bamfield's golden, catlike eyes narrowed on her with vague suspicion. Fingers, red, long and tapered as talons, dug possessively into Matthew's arm.

"Oh, darling, I think we qualify as more than friends, don't you?" She twisted her hand so that the large diamond on her ring finger winked in the moonlight. "And what exactly is your relationship with Miss Marlowe? Are you friends, as well?"

Every word came out of that perfect bow of a mouth loaded with a prying kind of jealousy. Her face was the face of an actress, molded into friendly, curious lines, but her eyes were not friendly at all.

"Mr. Blake is my employer," Charity said stiffly, saving Matthew the embarrassment of having to come up with a reply, and herself the embarrassment of having to hear it. "Now, if you'll excuse me, good night."

She looked at the clock when she got in. It was ten o'clock. She had been up for five hours. And she was absolutely exhausted. She wondered if she was getting sick.

If this was what Mandy happily referred to as romance, she decided that being an intern at a busy inner-city hospital was marginally less stressful.

It wasn't romance, anyway. It was...confusion. It was liking someone one minute and hating them the next. It was feeling attracted, and humiliated by that attraction. It was feeling out of control. It was feeling a deep ache of loss for something she had never had in the first place. These feeling were baffling and bewitching. And exhausting.

It occurred to her, just before she went to sleep, that she disliked Miss Sandra Bamfield as much as she had ever disliked anyone...except maybe Tommy Bellinger.

She wanted to think that Matthew deserved better, but he seemed to be rather enjoying the puzzling little game of hearts that was being played. Maybe he enjoyed playing it light and loose. Maybe it was all just a game to him, these stirring pulses and loaded glances, and chemical reactions.

Maybe he deserved a phony like that. Somebody as skilled at these intricate dances of the mind as he was.

And that certainly wasn't Charity. She wasn't even *fun,* and she didn't know how to do a dance of any sort.

It was not turning out to be the kind of summer she had intended. She sighed. Did anything really turn out the way human beings so carefully planned?

CHARITY ENJOYED her two days off. She had found a little beach not far from the lodge, but hard enough to reach that she was mostly by herself. She swam and read and sat in the sun...about as close as she had come to getting what she'd imagined for her one shining summer. She didn't see Matthew. Or Mandy. Nelson, having appointed her Anpetuwi's own version of "Dear Abby," took the trouble to seek her out to consult her about a problem he was having with the chambermaid, Billie.

So she was surprised, and vaguely annoyed, to see Sandra Bamfield picking her way cautiously over the large rocks that had to be scaled to get to the privacy of this particular beach.

She arrived, obviously in something of a temper, though she tried to hide it.

"My," she gasped, "all that work, for this?" Uninvited, she lay down her towel a very short distance from

Charity's and began to sort through an obscenely large bag, pulling out a variety of beauty products.

"I know you're the one," Sandra informed her, not looking at her, but rubbing cream into her skin in tiny circles.

"Pardon?"

"The one he was locked in the closet with the night I arrived."

Charity was thankful for the sunglasses that shielded her surprise from the other woman's prying eyes. Privately she wondered exactly what the gossip surrounding that incident was.

"Yes, it was an unfortunate accident," she said levelly. She picked up her book.

Sandra did not take the hint.

"Does he meet you here?"

"I beg your pardon?" Charity asked, shoving the sunglasses up onto her hair, and staring at Sandra with astonishment.

"I just wondered why somebody would bother to come way over here, unless they were meeting someone, privately... or hoping someone might take the hint and follow them."

"I come over here because I like to be alone," Charity said firmly. She dropped her glasses back onto her nose, and lifted her book.

"Oh, save it," Sandra said airily. "I know you're not really reading that book. You just think it looks good to be seen with books that nobody can pronounce the name of. You probably can't pronounce it yourself."

She knew this woman had reminded her of Tommy Bellinger! And she had learned long ago how to defuse the Tommy Bellingers of the world. She had an M.D.

behind her name, and she didn't have to prove anything to anyone.

"You're absolutely right," she said cheerfully. She rolled over on her side, and immediately immersed herself in the book, ignoring all the disgruntled settling-in noises Sandra was making.

"He's mine. I've come a long way to make a reconciliation with him, and I don't want interference from some snooty cocktail waitress. I can tell he's quite taken with you, for some reason."

Charity didn't answer. Unfortunately, pity for that poor pathetic creature began to creep into her kind heart. She rolled back over and regarded Sandra.

They must have been close to the same age, but Sandra looked very young, like a petulant child wearing the costume of a grown woman. There was fear and insecurity in those heavily made-up eyes.

"Sandra, I don't know Matthew all that well. I certainly don't know you." She recognized that her doctor voice had come out. Her "Dear Abby" voice, Nelson would call it. It was a voice that was a nice combination of wisdom, authority and compassion, and people generally listened to it. "I don't presume to know the kinds of problems you have experienced as a couple, but I must say that jealousy is unattractive. No one wants to feel owned by another person, and perhaps what Matthew needs from you is some breathing space, some freedom, a demonstration of trust in him."

"He's talked to you about me?" Sandra said, her voice shrill and betrayed.

"No, he hasn't. Not at all."

But it was too late; Sandra was picking up her things, and shooting Charity murderous looks.

"I'm going to make him hate you," she promised.

Charity felt her heart go out to the other woman. Sandra looked normal—better than normal, actually. But her beautiful mask had just slipped, and underneath were fear and insecurity so deep that only a professional would be able to uproot them.

"You poor girl," she said with soft sympathy. She knew the terrible suffering that went with mental disorders like delusion and obsession, and the words just slipped out.

But it was absolutely the wrong thing to say.

"You're going to regret the day you ever laid eyes on Matthew," Sandra hissed.

Charity ruefully watched her walking way. Somehow she doubted whether sharing with Sandra the fact that she already did regret the day she'd first laid eyes on Matthew would be helpful to anyone.

She wondered how much of this side of Sandra Matthew knew about, if any of it. She knew people with mental disorders could often be extremely clever at concealing them.

She sighed. Another little dark cloud had appeared on the horizon of her summer.

CHAPTER EIGHT

A WEEK OF relative calm followed. Charity should have recognized it as the calm before the storm, but she didn't. Work kept her busy, and on several occasions she actually enjoyed her job. But she was still in the grip of a puzzling weariness, and she could barely walk by her couch without feeling compelled to drop down on it for a short nap. Still trying to make reality match with her fantasy, she took to napping on the beach in the afternoons.

A suspicion kept niggling at the back of her mind, but she kept pushing it away as more than she could deal with.

Matthew was still repairing damage from the windstorm, cutting fallen trees into logs for the lodge's many fireplaces. It was a job he seemed to be going after with a vengeance, despite the fact that the sizzling summer temperatures didn't exactly encourage the use of much firewood, and the lodge had not had a winter season for nearly ten years. The sound of his chainsaw started at dawn and didn't stop until dusk, at which point he started hauling the product of his day's labor into the woodshed. He never stopped in at the Susweca for refreshment after he was finished for the day.

Charity personally felt he was going farther and farther afield to find fallen trees, but that was his business. And the farther away, the better, anyway. He had a dismaying habit of pulling off his shirt as soon as he warmed up, and the sight of his bare and muscled torso shining with sweat was not something she dealt with rationally or easily.

Sandra moped. She wandered around the lodge, looking patently bored, refusing to take part in activities, and complaining about the service, the primitive facilities, and the lack of time Matthew had for her.

Mandy, as always, bounced through every day full of cheer and optimism, watching all the goings-on as if she had happened on front-row seats at the most enjoyable of soap operas. She was fond of making vague comments to Charity about everything being just fine, and weren't things progressing well, and everything would turn out exactly right.

Nelson had fallen head over heels in love with Billie, and had unofficially appointed Charity chief consultant of matters of the heart, which was about the biggest joke she had ever heard.

Guests came and went, totally unaware of the intricate weaving of human relationships all around them.

"I wonder why she stays?" Mandy mused one evening as she and Charity sat out on their rickety porch eating salads and sweating. "Billie says they don't even sleep together."

Charity nearly lost a mouthful of salad. "Mandy!"

"For gosh sake, for somebody who knows the human anatomy inside and out, you're awfully prim, Charity. Anyway, he's taken to disappearing every morning at dawn and not returning until he's exhausted. He doesn't spend any time with her. Why doesn't she take the hint?"

"Unfortunately," Charity said, unable to feign complete indifference to the topic, "I suspect the more he rejects her, the more her self-esteem becomes tied up in winning him over."

"Hey, that's pretty good, Doc," Mandy said with genuine appreciation.

"Mandy—"

"Right. Don't call you Doc. She seems to hate *you* pretty thoroughly. I told you his attraction to you is obvious."

To everybody but me, maybe, Charity thought. Matthew seemed to avoid her as studiously as he avoided Sandra!

"She's made some really snide comments to some of the staff about you. Can you imagine what she must say to Matthew?"

"That I'm a two-headed yellow-bellied adulteress serving the clients poisoned drinks—as slowly as I possibly can," Charity guessed with good humor.

"Aren't you frosted?"

"No," Charity said, growing serious. "Mandy, she's not a bad person so much as a sick one. She wants to believe *I'm* the reason Matthew isn't returning her affections. She wants to believe that, if I weren't around, everything would be all right between them."

Mandy gave her red curls a shocked shake. "Gosh, Charity, you genuinely care about her, don't you?"

"I guess that's why I've made the choices I've made, Mandy. I care about people. And I especially seem to care about the sick ones. Please, don't be mean to her on my behalf. She has enough problems as it is."

"Does this mean I have go and retrieve the toad from her bed?"

Charity laughed and stretched. It was nice to be around Mandy. It was good to discuss other people's problems. It kept her mind off her own—like the disturbing fact that her period was now several days late.

That night, walking down to the lodge to do her shift, she was surprised to see Matthew deep in discussion with two members of the Royal Canadian Mounted Police.

He was just saying goodbye to them as she drew up.

"Charity, I'd like to speak to you."

Her silly heart went wild. She hadn't spoken to Matthew in a long time. It seemed to her that when he spotted her he usually did a quick about-face, which, to be fair, was also how she responded to seeing him.

"I hope there hasn't been any kind of trouble," she said, watching the policemen disappear up the path. She turned her attention back to him, and smiled, a bit uncertainly. "It's really easy to believe, here, that we aren't a part of the real world, isn't it?"

She immediately felt foolish for the schoolgirlish remark. Not part of the real world? Where life was complicated by worries of pregnancy and a jealous girlfriend, and an indifferent man who made your heart go crazy? How *real* did she want it exactly?

"It has seemed like that," he said somberly, looking off into the distance. "No murders, or burglaries, no assaults. A place apart from the rest of the world. Until now, anyway. Some of my grandmother's jewelry has gone missing. I just wanted to alert the staff in case any of you have seen or heard anything suspicious."

The wild beating of her heart steadied. She felt a rush of disappointment. All he wanted was to discuss business, and that was good. That was safe. He was being mature and rational.

She looked into his eyes. They were steady on her face, and they certainly weren't discussing business. They were smoking with pent-up longing.

"I'm terribly sorry about your grandmother's jewelry," Charity said, verbally scampering back to safe ground as fast as she could. She hesitated. "But, given your grandmother's absentmindedness, don't you think it might have been a little premature to call in the police?"

"I don't think misplacing twenty thousand dollars' worth of jewelry is quite in the same category as forgetting your glasses are hanging from a chain around your neck."

Charity gasped. "What was she doing with that kind of jewelry here?"

"I guess, rather like you, she feels this place is magical. Apart from the world. As if nothing bad happens here." There was a certain bitter anger in his voice, but it was obvious that it was caused by a tenderness for his grandmother. He had wanted her to be able to keep her illusions. In some way, he probably felt he had failed her.

"I'm sure the jewelry has just been misplaced, and not stolen, Matthew." She said it softly, but with certainty.

"How can you be so sure?"

"I don't know for sure. But there is a peace in the air here... a feeling of well-being." She blushed. She was probably sounding hopelessly naive again.

But Matthew smiled, his teeth white and strong and so sensuous that they sent a shiver up her spine. "My mother used to say that."

Now she reminded him of his mother!

She'd rather be seen as hopelessly naive, and she voiced her feelings, suddenly not caring if she did seem that way. "Your mother was right. And even, God forbid, if the jewelry was taken, you watch it, it will turn around and something really good will come out of it."

"You little Pollyanna," he said with a snort of derisive laughter, but the look in his eyes was not derisive. It was faintly... wistful. As if, like her, he could not be in her company without remembering.

What did he remember? Shared laughter? Playful conversation? Kisses, hot and sultry as a summer night? Skin touching skin, like satin on silk?

"I've seen you and Nelson walking in the woods together." He said this with a certain measured diffidence, as though it meant nothing at all to him, and was just a casual observation. But again, his eyes, those dark blue eyes, said something else.

"He's appointed me chief adviser on affairs of the heart. Lord knows why," she said lightly. "It is not an area of expertise for me."

"You mean he isn't still harboring that schoolboy crush on you?"

Faint as it was, was that relief in his voice? Why was her own heart starting to beat so hard again, frantically, as if it was trying to tell her something she could not or would not hear?

"No, I'm afraid I dashed that at dinner that night. I'm not exactly the stuff that can nurture a man's fantasies for any length of time."

"Don't underestimate yourself," he said darkly.

And then it was there, that which they so carefully avoided. The chemistry was back, right between them, like a huge black cauldron, bubbling and streaming. But did it hold menace or magic? Whatever, it was there, waiting, waiting, waiting—for one ingredient to complete it, to set off a reaction that might never stop. What would that ingredient be?

A touch, perhaps. Or eyes held a moment too long. Or an errant tongue nervously touching lips.

He jammed his hands deep into his pockets as if to prevent himself from reaching out, touching her, taking her...

She forced words over the hard hammering of her heart. "And how is Sandra's visit going?" she asked, desperately, trying to get some sort of shield up between them.

"It's going," he muttered. "And the sooner it goes, the better."

But she had succeeded in erecting the shield between them. His jaw tightened and his features looked suddenly cool and remote.

"I'm going to be late for work," she said nervously.

He stepped back from her, abruptly. "We wouldn't want that," he said smoothly, and for a moment the shield came crashing back down, because his eyes wanted exactly that. His eyes were kissing her lips and her neck, and her ears. His eyes wanted her to be very late for work indeed.

She brushed by him and dashed up the stairs of the lodge. It was only then that she saw Sandra, standing concealed in the shadow of the eaves. Sandra smiled at her with such malignant dislike that she shivered.

SOMEHOW, over the running water, she finally heard the loud knocking on the cabin door. She was trying to wash her hair in the sink, and she straightened, wrapped a towel around her dripping hair, pulled her housecoat tight and marched to the door.

She was going to tell Nelson enough was enough. She didn't know if women preferred poetry or flowers or a night at the movies. She didn't know anything about falling in love, let alone falling in love on a budget, as Nelson put it. Her own heart was in such a state of turmoil that she couldn't possibly give him one more piece of advice. And she couldn't listen to him anymore, either, talking in low, confused tones about all the pain and pathos he was feeling, mixed with the glory and delight. His innocent words touched sensitive spots within her own heart.

Nelson was going to have to fumble through on his own—just as she was fumbling through each day, holding her breath hoping to see him, talk to Matthew... trying to understand this hunger inside her.

"Hunger" was the only word that would describe it. A physical longing so strong that it seemed her very survival must be linked to it. A longing to touch him. To be touched by him. To talk to him. To hear the music of his laughter. To walk with him. To hold his hand. To peel his clothing from him...

How she envied Billie and Nelson the relative normality of their relationship. The fact that they walked hand in hand, and exchanged shy and wondering glances, and had little squabbles, and not so little jealousies.

Whereas she lived in a fantasy of her own making. She did not have a relationship with Matthew. She had a few tawdry memories—and the constant presence of the woman who wanted to be his wife to deal with.

She could not even define her feelings. Did not want to. She felt desperate and despairing enough without adding the word "love" to this already hopelessly tangled equation.

She told herself she was just feeling a biological urge. Perfectly natural. Perfectly human. A female of the species, at her particular age, finally acknowledging biological programming—her body insisting she do the things bodies were designed to do.

"All right," she called, "I'm coming."

She swung open the door, expecting Nelson. The shock of seeing Matthew standing there took her breath away.

But there was something so grim, so untouchable in the set of his face that there was a pause in the upward fluttering of her heart—a pause, and then a downward plunge to earth.

"What's the matter, Matthew?"

"What makes you think that something is the matter?" He leaned a big shoulder against the doorjamb, and his eyes swept her. A lip turned up at the towel in her hair, as if he was remembering that first time they'd seen each other, but the quirk of that lip was cruel.

"What do you want, Matthew?" She folded her arms over her chest, uncomfortably aware of the shabbiness of her old pink housecoat, uncomfortably aware of an anger sizzling at the back of those eyes.

Mrs. Foster had told them Matthew was a bad-tempered boy, and she'd certainly been right about the bad-tempered part, though this was no boy standing here looking at her with such menace.

"You know what I want," he said harshly.

She gasped, only because she knew what she wanted from him. She knew it kept her awake these hot nights, restless with a deep and hard yearning that never eased, never went away. She scanned his face. No, that was not what he was saying.

"I want the jewelry, Charity."

"The jewelry?" His answer was so far from the murmuring of her own mind that she could not comprehend what he was saying. "What jewelry?"

"Don't play the innocent with me. You tried to convince me it had been misplaced. You tried to convince me not to involve the police."

"You mean your grandmother's jewelry?" she asked with stunned disbelief.

"No, the Crown jewels. Have you got those, too?"

"Matthew, I don't have your grandmother's—"

"Oh, stop it," he snapped. "I got an anonymous note saying you wore one of her rings on your shift last night."

"That's ridiculous," she said. She had been shrinking away from his anger and distaste, but now she was coming back, a hot fury of her own growing within her. How dared he question her integrity, the very fabric her entire being was built around?

She stabbed an angry finger into his chest. "Have you ever seen me wear jewelry of any kind, Matthew? Think about it!"

Something pierced his anger. A puzzlement. "No, I guess I haven't." But his tone was still guarded and still edged with hostility.

"And do you really think that if I had taken something of your grandmother's I would be stupid enough to wear it to work?"

He frowned.

"And do you really think if I had twenty thousand dollars' worth of jewelry I'd still be here? Still hanging out as a cocktail waitress?"

The bubble of his anger had burst, and he stood looking at her, doubt shading the blue of his eyes now.

"How could you?" she demanded, her voice low with contempt. "How could you ever accuse me of something so totally. . . impossible!"

"Look, lady, nothing about you has measured up from the beginning. You don't look like a woman who would falsify a document to get a job, but you did. Your eyes are all innocence, but your lips are pure fire. You talk like a bloody Rhodes scholar, and you're slinging drinks at a lounge."

His tone suddenly softened. "I don't understand you, Charity. For one insane moment, it made sense. Ah, a glamorous jewel thief. That explains it. The falsified application, all the contradictions, all the things I don't understand."

He shook his head, as if clearing it. "I'm sorry. I acted on impulse. I got the note, and I didn't even think..."

His voice trailed away, rough with apology. She tried to turn away from him, but his hand, strong and hard, cupped her chin before she could.

"Oh, Lord, Charity, please don't cry."

But she couldn't help it; the silent tears coursed out of her eyes and cascaded down her cheeks as she stared up at him, the betrayal wrenching at her heart.

"Just leave me alone," she croaked, smacking his hand down from her chin. Again she tried to turn from him, but again strong hands stopped her. This time they rested on her shoulders, then pulled her with gentle and insistent strength into the wall of his chest.

"I'm sorry," he said again, and the floodgates really opened, and she began to cry for all the bewilderment of feelings he had caused in her.

"How could you think it was me?" she whispered, her voice breaking. "How could you?"

"I don't think I did think," he admitted softly. "I don't think I really believed it for one second. It just gave me an excuse to come charging up here."

Again she tried to break away. The tears were drying now. Her pride was rearing up inside her. "Well, you can just charge back down again!"

His arms held, though now she had wedged her hands between her breasts and the hard wall of his chest and was pushing away from him with all her might.

"Charity, I don't think clearly as soon as you come into the picture. Passion starts to muddle my thinking. Even when I was charging up here full of righteousness, part of me was thinking of this."

His lips brushed hers, lightly, like a butterfly's wing.

"Only," he whispered, "it was going to be hard and punishing. More like this." And his lips took hers again, but they were not hard and punishing. They were exquisitely gentle, exploring, discovering . . . worshiping. His tongue, hot and sweet, tempted open her lips and slipped into her mouth.

By the time he had finished that, she was nearly faint with desire.

"I think," he murmured softly, "I was looking for an excuse to shake you . . ." Instead his arms tightened around her, drawing her softness back into his hardness. "To touch you . . . In my imagination, I was going to pick you up in a fury of emotion, toss you down on that bed—"

He picked her up with exquisite gentleness, kissed her cheeks, laid her gently on the bed, and lay down on it beside her, his hands pulling her body close to his.

"—I was going to rip your clothes from you—" His hands sought the belt of her housecoat, and his every movement seemed to be tempered with respect. He tugged it free, and her housecoat gaped open, revealing the creamy silk of her breasts.

"—and then I was going to kiss you here...and here." His lips trailed fire down her breasts. "You see," he murmured, "I wanted to believe it, so I could have an excuse to take what I wanted in fury, instead of reaching out of my confusion and asking for what I wanted—"

"Take what you want," she whispered, the tears still streaming down her face. But they were different tears now, gentled with understanding and forgiveness.

"No," he whispered. "I won't take anything. Only give. And only with your permission. May I make love to you, Charity?"

"Yes," she whispered, and as his heated lips touched again the silken surface of her skin she arched against him. "Yes," she cried, an affirmation of life itself. "Yes."

He went slowly, anointing every inch of her skin with kisses, tender nips, the rough surface of his tongue. She was shivering with delight and pent-up desire. She tried to give back, but he stayed her with his somber eyes and his sultry mouth.

Finally, she could bear his one-sided possession no longer. Despite his trying to stop her, her hungry kiss sought his mouth, tasted him and tested him. Her hands stroked the silk of his skin with bold pleasure. She gave herself over completely to sensation.

With a sigh of utter defeat and utter pleasure, he accepted her mouth and her hands returning his gifts to him.

The gentleness faded. They were two starving people in the midst of a feast of sensation. There was a throbbing urgency developing in the way they touched, a desperation in their kisses; the yearning for fulfilment that had been growing in her since this man had first taken her was now a scream deep inside her, aching for him, crying for him, sobbing for him.

They came together, their passion so out of control that there was a certain violence to it, a wildness, a drive beyond reason. It was a total letting go. For two people who both were always in control, this was something of a miracle—to let go of control completely—to trust enough that they were both hurled into the abyss of pure sensation, pure feeling. Skin and sweat and scent and desire became the whole world. There was nothing left of it but these things, as with cries of animal passion they allowed the storm that had brewed around them all summer to reach its thunderous climax.

She began to shake with reaction as soon as it was done. Her hair was sweat-soaked, and so was her skin. Tenderly he touched her, kissed her lips, not with passion now, but with a delicate reverence, as if he were kissing the fragile bloom of a rare flower.

He pulled them both under the blanket, cradled her to him, crooned words that meant nothing in her ear, kissed new tears from her cheeks. And the new tears were for the absolute tenderness she had seen in his eyes.

She smiled with soft, sweet knowing. She had told him something good would come out of that missing jewelry, but she had had no idea of just how wonderful it was going to be.

They slept and she awoke to a tongue exploring the delicate curve of her ear.

"I hate to bring the real world into this, but is your roommate going to pop in at any second?"

She turned in his arms so she could see him. What she saw took her breath away. He was propped up on one elbow, his dark hair sweat-curled, his eyes gleaming with desire, his naked chest and arms magnificent in their absolute masculinity.

"Mandy took one of her more ambitious hikes out today. She won't be back for hours."

"Wonderful," he murmured, touching a tender spot on her neck, and growling a playful warning when she flinched away from him.

But the flinch was not because he had touched a tender spot on her neck. It was because a tender spot on her soul was regaining consciousness.

Yes, she was sure of the great passion he felt for her. She was even aware of the tenderness in his eyes as he looked at her.

But she needed something more than that. She needed him to love her. She needed him to be ready to make some sort of commitment to her. When had this happened to her?

Love. She had avoided that word all summer, and yet it didn't matter. Words only represented reality. They were only symbols. She had not used the word, but it didn't matter. What that word represented had begun to grow in her from almost the very first moment she had seen him. Denying it had not stopped it from growing. Trying to run from it had not stopped it, either.

Against her will and her better judgment, she had fallen in love.

And if that word, if that tiny little word didn't really mean anything, why did it hurt so much that he hadn't used it?

"Let's have a shower together," he muttered thickly in her ear.

She wanted to say no. The spirit was willing. But the flesh was weak.

One last encounter. She would allow herself a few more hours with him, and then she would practice self-discipline. Then she would find her pride and not indulge in this kind of behavior when it had no future.

They went into the bathroom together; he adjusted the taps and then pulled her under the steaming water with him.

His skin was glistening and smooth. Hesitantly she picked up the soap and began to soap the expanse of his chest, while he looked down at her.

His skin, combined with the slippery texture of the soap, seemed to come alive under her hands. She soaped all of him, delighting in his textures and curves, delighting in what her touch did to his body.

And then he took the soap from her, and made her stand still under the pummeling water, while very slowly he soaped her, and used the flannel to take the soap away. She was shivering uncontrollably, but not because she was cold. That ache that she thought had been satiated for all time was back within her.

He dropped the soap and wrapped his arms around her, they slid against each other, their skin slippery and sensual. His lips caught her as the water cascaded around them, and it was like being kissed under a waterfall.

He reached behind him, with one hand, the other still pressed into the small of her back, and turned off the water.

They stood, clothed only in steam, their lips locked together. Slowly he eased himself onto the side of the tub, drawing her down with him. She sat, straddling him, while his hands touched and teased and caressed.

And then, when he had taunted her and tempted her until she was shaking with need, with easy strength he lifted her, and put her back down so that his throbbing masculinity was nestled inside the warm and inviting hollow of her body.

They made love slowly and with deep appreciation of the way their bodies fitted together perfectly, like pieces of a perfect puzzle. Their previous urgency was exhausted, and this time it was long and slow, punctuated with breathless laughter and husky words of endearment. This time there was a deep awareness of each other, an awareness of the sacredness of this kind of union. Finally, with a tensing of their whole souls, they exploded into the moment that brought utter fulfilment.

"I never would have thought—" she said, at last, peeking up at him with dazed eyes. "The side of the bathtub. I mean—"

But he quieted her with gentle lips, untangled their limbs and they stood up, pressed into each other.

"Your goose bumps are getting goose bumps," he said gently. "I'll get you a towel."

"That closet behind you."

He opened the tiny cupboard, pulled out a thick towel and passed it to her. As he yanked one out for himself, something clattered loudly to the floor.

Charity stared, stunned, at the open, upside-down jewelry box on her bathroom floor, and at the necklace that winked up at her, looking like a dozen teardrops strung together on a web of silver.

CHAPTER NINE

A NERVOUS LAUGH escaped Charity. Somehow, when she had planned her perfect summer, she had never imagined a scenario like this. Here she was, buck-naked, in her bathroom with an equally undressed man, with twenty thousand dollars' worth of jewelry scattered on the floor between them.

Stolen jewelry.

Matthew glanced at her, his expression unreadable. He cinched his towel around his hips, then bent and scooped up the jewelry as if it were junk. He shoved it back into the box and snapped down the lid viciously.

She wrapped her own towel around herself. Her mixed-up mind wondered if this was yet another of Mandy's crazy schemes. Where there was trouble, usually Mandy was not far behind.

"Did you do it, Charity?" There was great pain in his voice.

"How can you even ask?" she whispered, her eyes filming over. "Especially after that."

"Unfortunately, *that* did not exactly clarify my thinking. It made it cloudier than ever where you are concerned. Please just answer me. Did you do it?"

"No." She said it simply and quietly, her eyes meeting his without flinching.

He studied her for a long time, then reached out and touched a wet strand of her hair. Then he nodded, almost curtly, wheeled and left her standing in the bathroom all alone.

Within minutes she heard the front door of the cabin slam shut and she knew he was gone. She suddenly felt nauseous, and went to the sink and heaved uncontrollably.

She went and sat, shaken, on the edge of her bed. She did not know if he had believed her. But she did know one thing. She had to leave. There was little doubt in her mind that she was pregnant.

When Mandy came in, Charity was just closing the lid on her suitcase, the little cabin stripped bare of her belongings. As soon as she saw Mandy's face she burst into tears.

Mandy rushed over, and made her sit down on the couch. She put a motherly arm around her shoulder, and the whole story, except the part about being almost certain she was pregnant, came spilling out.

"Mrs. Foster's jewels were in our bathroom closet? Wow! Isn't it exciting? Just like a mystery novel!"

"M-M-M-Mandy, d-did you put them there?"

"Me? You think I'm a jewel thief? That hurts, Charity!" Mandy's hurt lasted all of about thirty seconds. "But you do see how it's possible to really, really care about someone and still harbour some little doubt about them? I mean, you know me better than anyone in the world, you probably love me better than anyone in the world, but you still never *know* another person one hundred percent."

"I guess I do see that," Charity said grudgingly. "I know you're not a jewel thief, Mandy, but I also know you sometimes act impulsively, thinking it's okay to do something that's wrong if you have the right motive."

"And because of that application form, Matthew thinks that you're just like me—that you'll stretch the rules a bit to get what you want. If only he knew you never break the rules, Dudley Do-Right. Charity, I should have come clean on that right away. I'm ashamed of myself."

"Thinking I would stretch the rules to suit myself is very different from thinking I would be so consumed by greed that I would commit a felony."

"Come on. Lighten up. He didn't actually say he didn't believe you, right?"

"And he didn't actually say he did believe me, either. But he came here thinking I had that jewelry, and then it fell right out of my closet. What would you think, given those circumstances?"

"I would think no jewel thief worth her salt would send a man directly to the hiding spot—no matter how high above the ground she was floating."

"He won't think of that."

"Why not? He's an awfully smart man. That's why I think the two of you are such a good match."

"He won't think of it because . . . because he doesn't think clearly about me."

Mandy gave a warm laugh. "Do you hear what you're saying, girl? What does it mean to you when a man isn't thinking clearly?"

"That he's had too much to drink, or a bad hit on the head," Charity said stubbornly.

"Get your brain out of the emergency ward. What does it mean if he hadn't had too much to drink or a bad hit on the head?"

"What does it matter? It's over. I have to leave this place while I have an ounce of pride and sanity left."

"But you can't! If you leave now, you'll look guilty for sure."

"If he doesn't know I'm not guilty, there's no chance of us ever working anything out . . . and if there's no chance, I just can't stay."

"How are you going to know what he thinks if you don't stay? Charity, take my word for it. This is a critical moment in this relationship. It's not him you're running from. It's yourself. You've been given an invitation to the most magnificent show in the world. You've been given an invitation to fall in love. You're scared to death. Of course you are. But don't run, Charity. Don't run from this."

"Mandy, I haven't exactly seen you throwing yourself on the altar of love."

Something changed in Mandy's face. It was a look Charity had never seen before. Total and abject sadness clouded those lovely little features.

"I got my invitation, once," Mandy said. "Right here. Last summer. His name was Gus. He was ten years older than me, and homely as a hedge fence, and the lodge handyman. He made me laugh like no one on earth has ever made me laugh. I could talk to him, like no one else. I always felt safe and happy with him. He was humble and wise. He asked me to marry him, and you know, my heart said yes, this is the one. But my head said I wanted something else. I wanted a fairy tale. Someone younger and more handsome and with a little more stature in the world. I thought I could look around a bit more, and that Gus would always be there if I changed my mind."

Mandy had started to cry. "But he wasn't. He died in a car accident last winter. Sometimes you only get one invitation to this particular dance, Charity. Take it."

"Mandy, why didn't you ever say anything?"

"It was a deep and private grief," Mandy said, wiping at her eyes. "Don't miss your chance to dance, Charity."

"It's not quite the same. Matthew Blake hasn't invited me to do anything."

"Life is inviting you to do something! Are you blind?"

"I guess so."

"It's her," Mandy said, suddenly, quietly. "It's her!" she crowed with delight.

"What?" That was Mandy, from pathos to pleasure in the blink of an eye.

"Who is staying with Mrs. Foster? For heaven's sake, who has access to all her jewelry?"

For a moment Charity's mind grappled with the too swift change of topic, but then the light went on. "Oh," she said softly.

"And who has a grudge the size of Mount Everest against you?"

"Sandra."

"Of course," Mandy said. "This is so much fun. You and Matthew are the smart ones, and you couldn't even see the noses in front of your faces. And then a dummy like me comes along—"

"You're not a dummy."

"—and solves the whole mystery. You and Matthew have it for each other so bad you probably couldn't add two and two together."

"I have it bad," Charity said morosely. "I can't speak for him. And I really can't wait around to find out if I suffer unrequited love. I have to go."

"Don't go. Give it a chance."

"I have given it a chance. Absolutely nothing has happened."

"You call this afternoon nothing?"

"No. This afternoon was the capper. The man I have been foolish enough to fall for is incapable of trusting me."

"You're just jumping to conclusions, but if you go now he'll think you did it."

"I don't care. Let him stick the RCMP on me, if he wants. I'm sure the police would figure out quickly enough that I'm hardly the criminal type."

"It wouldn't make a very good start for your career if there was any kind of publicity."

"I don't care," she said stubbornly, but even as she said the words she knew they weren't a hundred percent true.

"You can't leave the lodge in the lurch like that, Charity," Mandy told her sternly. "It's not like you to run away from your responsibilities. You're supposed to be at work in less than an hour. What about that?"

"Nelson will do it. He's better at it than me, anyway."

"Charity, I have never seen you so self-pitying. And Nelson won't do it, because he's not here. He took Billie to a movie."

"You do it, then."

"No."

"I don't care who does it."

"Yes, you do. Just stay until we find a replacement for you, Charity. Please. It would reflect really badly on me if you left without notice. You can avoid Matthew. I've noticed you're pretty good at that, anyway. And maybe this will all blow over..."

Charity sighed. The part Mandy didn't know about wasn't going to blow over. But then what was a few more days? She didn't want to look as if she was running away, after all.

"I'll stay," she announced coolly. "Until the end of the week. That's all."

"That'll be enough," Mandy said happily.

"And there's a condition."

"What's that?"

"That you don't interfere in any way. That you don't take it upon yourself to plead my case or to point an accusing finger at Sandra."

"But why not?" Mandy wailed.

"Because if he can't see it himself, it's worthless. Do you understand?"

"Yes," Mandy said glumly. "Unfortunately, I do."

HER SHIFT WAS half over, but Charity was sorry she had agreed to do it. She seemed abnormally sensitive to the smoke smells and her stomach was rolling uncomfortably. Even the smell of some of the drinks was nauseating her, her sense of smell seeming far keener than normal. Her legs seemed oddly wobbly as well, and she realized that she might not be able to keep her obligation to Mandy, after all.

Suddenly the doors to the lounge burst open.

Sandra stood there, her eyes rolling with fear, her complexion pasty under all that makeup.

"Is there a doctor here?" she cried. "We need a doctor right away!"

Charity dropped her tray on the nearest table. Ignoring startled looks, she raced over to the frightened young woman and took her shoulders in both her hands. She could feel Sandra trembling.

"Doctor," Sandra repeated, dazedly. "We need—"

"Where?" she snapped.

"The dining room. Matthew ate—"

But it was as if she already knew, had known the moment that Sandra had pushed through those doors. An anaphylactic reaction was a desperate emergency, and delays could prove fatal.

She ran through the doors to the dining room. She nearly knocked over Nelson, who was just heading toward the lounge, his arm around Billie's shoulder.

"Nelson. There's a doctor's bag under my bed in my cabin. Get it. *Now.*"

He gaped at her. "A doctor's—"

"Now!" she shouted over her shoulder.

There was a crowd of people milling around, and she pushed through them impatiently. "I'm a doctor. Let me through."

He was lying on the floor, already inert, his face pale, his breathing wheezing and labored. Mrs. Foster was beside him, holding his hand and crying.

"How long has he been like this?" Charity asked, crouching beside him. She knew that the more quickly the reaction happened, the more severe the shock to his system. She also knew that he could die within five minutes.

Mrs. Foster thankfully reached into the part of her brain that wasn't addled. "It was two or three minutes before he collapsed. He's been like this only for about thirty seconds. Charity, dear, we need a doctor," she whispered. "Terrible allergy. He's going to die if we don't get help."

Charity finished taking Matthew's pulse. It was nearly imperceptible. Matthew was obviously having respiratory and cardiovascular manifestations of anaphylaxis.

Sandra had just arrived back in time to hear Mrs. Foster's grim assessment of the situation. "Die?" she screamed hysterically.

"Sandra, go to his room. He's got to have an allergy kit there. Find it."

"But I don't know what it looks like."

"Go!" She had given the instruction more to get the hysterical woman out of her hair, since she already knew her medical bag was on the way. "Does anyone here have a Benadryl?"

A package was passed to her. The antihistamine would have little value, but it might slow the reaction marginally until her medical kit or the allergy kit arrived. If she could just keep that swelling airway open! She placed a capsule under his tongue.

For a shocked second she was very aware that this was the mouth that only hours before had been kissing her, making her feel things she had never felt. "Sometimes you only get one invitation to this particular dance, Charity. Take it..."

She snapped herself out of it. She knew she could not afford to lose her professional edge by thinking of him personally. With the most supreme effort she had ever made, she thought of him as the patient.

Matthew's breathing stopped.

And in that instant, way in the back of her mind, Charity knew the full breadth and depth of her love for this man.

She tore open his shirt and began cardiopulmonary resuscitation. Fifteen chest compressions. Two breaths, hard into his mouth, trying to force air through that badly swollen airway.

"Almonds in cake," Mrs. Foster was muttering. "He's always so careful. He asked, and the waitress told him no. He'd usually smell it, you know. So distracted today. So distracted. This dreadful business with the jewelry..."

The words were going into Charity's brain but she wasn't really registering them, her focus was so concentrated on the rhythm of the CPR. She was already sweating with exertion. Where was Nelson?

Then he was there, and that beautiful black bag was beside her.

Sandra came back screaming that she couldn't find the other kit.

"Get Sandra out of here," she ordered, that high-pitched wailing piercing her consciousness, and scraping across her already too taut nerves. "Does anybody else do CPR?"

"I took a course," Nelson said, "but—"

"Take over," she ordered, watching him out of the corner of her eye. Some kind soul had forsaken the drama to escort Sandra out of the room and comfort her. Nelson, thank God, knew what he was doing.

Quickly she opened the bag and found her epinephrine. Ideally, at this late stage, he should be given it intravenously, but there was no intravenous here. She prepared an injection, made her decision, and shot the drug into him intramuscularly. She vigorously massaged the area to distribute the drug through his body more quickly. Nelson continued CPR. Medically, there was nothing left to do. She found herself praying, the only thing she did consistently as a physician that could ever be called unprofessional.

Within seconds his eyes fluttered open, and she looked deep into those beloved blue depths. The relief crashed in around her. She realized that part of the wailing she was hearing was a siren. Someone had called an ambulance, and it must be coming down the service road now.

"Charity," he whispered thickly. "What—?"

"Don't try to talk just yet," she advised him. "You've had an anaphylactic reaction."

"I know...the cake. But what are you...?" His eyes, still confused, took in the needle in her hand, the bag beside her. And then a slow smile creased his features.

"I said I'd know," he informed her. "Remember?"

"Remember? No. Matthew, it's not important right now."

He closed his eyes, but he was still smiling. "Dr. Marlowe. Dr. Charity Marlowe. A perfect fit."

Two burly ambulance attendants were pushing through. She had them put an oxygen mask over Matthew's face immediately. Only then did she briefly introduce herself. She instructed them on what had happened and what she had done, and what she recommended be done next. Matthew would need to be hospitalized at least overnight where he could receive further epinephrine if necessary, and his vital signs could be monitored.

Sandra had come back into the room, and somehow she was at Matthew's side, holding his hand and weeping.

"It's okay, darling," he murmured thickly.

Charity trailed after the crowd out to the ambulance. She watched Sandra squeeze in with him. All these people were smacking her on the back, and touching her and congratulating her, and expressing surprise and delight. There was always a sort of universal coming together when an emergency was averted, when a human life was saved.

But she felt oddly detached from it, eager to be away from these happy people.

Nelson seemed to sense it, and protectively he put his arm around her shoulder, walked her, supporting her heavily, up to her cabin.

And it was Nelson who held her when her own shock set in and she quietly wept. She had come so close to losing the man she loved. And for one moment, when his eyes had opened and he had looked at her, she had been so sure that he had loved her back.

But it had been Sandra he'd called darling. Maybe it was she who'd been deluding herself about the state of his and Sandra's relationship, and not the other way around.

"Wow!" Nelson kept saying. "A doctor. Wait until I tell my friends I had a date with a doctor this summer."

Hours later, she was still up, still pacing restlessly around her small cabin trying not to wake Mandy. The experience had given her her own shot of adrenalin and sleep was unthinkable.

Deep in the night, there was a knock on the door.

Sandra stood there. "Can I speak to you?"

Charity slipped out of the door.

"Is he all right?" she asked anxiously.

"Yes, he's fine. I suppose I should thank you." The words were said tightly and with reluctance.

"I don't see why," Charity said. "I did my job. That's all."

"But that isn't all, is it?"

"I don't know what you mean."

"You love him. It was written all over your face. Especially when it was me he turned to, me he called darling."

Charity could feel the blood draining from her face.

"We've settled our differences, you know. In a way, this is just what he needed to make him realize how much he cared about me."

Charity's tired mind felt overloaded. She was not sure if what she was hearing was truth or lies, or a mixture of both.

"You may think I fell apart and didn't handle myself very well."

"I don't think that at all," Charity said. "Most people don't face emergencies as a matter of course, and no one expects them to be anything but human."

"My reaction finally helped Matthew to understand how much I love him."

"Really?" Charity said, unable to keep the dry note from her voice.

"You know, you types never quite seem to get it."

"Get what?"

"What a man likes in a woman. Men like women who are weak and helpless. They like to feel strong and protective."

"I guess some of us 'types' have better things to do with our lives than dedicate ourselves to the attraction of the opposite sex." Again her tone was dry.

"For instance, your great heroism was most admirable, but I'm sure all Matthew would feel is emasculated by it."

"Emasculated?" Charity repeated with dull wonder.

"He doesn't even wear his medic-alert bracelet. What does that tell you about how he relates his illness to his masculinity?"

"I'm not sure."

"He doesn't want people to know, for heaven's sake. And he certainly doesn't want an attractive woman saving him. It's supposed to be the other way around."

"Perhaps I should send him a note of apology."

Sandra missed the tense humor in her voice. "I wouldn't bother. He was in a very bad state of mind about you when I left him."

"I saved his life!"

"Well, surely you didn't think that would take the sting out of the deception you've been practicing?"

"My deception?" Charity managed to croak.

"He feels as if you played him for a fool. Set him up to be a laughingstock. A doctor working as a waitress. It is really weird."

"How about if *you* don't talk to me about *weird,*" Charity said, with her first touch of impatience.

"What do you mean?" Sandra asked, widening her eyes innocently.

"I mean *I* didn't steal Mrs. Foster's jewels."

"Oh, that. You can't prove I did it, either," Sandra said coolly, with absolutely no recognition of wrong-doing in her voice.

"Sandra, don't you understand? That kind of jealous behavior isn't conducive to having a healthy, strong relationship. You need—"

"Look, *Doctor,* I'm not one of your patients, and I'm not going to listen to you tell me what I need. I need Matthew. And I got him. You didn't. Are you going to be pathetic about it?"

Charity knew there was no sense talking to Sandra. None at all. And she found it interesting that Sandra would project her own pathetic pursuit of Matthew onto someone else.

Or maybe it hadn't been so pathetic.

Things were not always as they appeared.

She went back into her cabin and firmly closed the door.

They knew she was a doctor now, and Mandy had already warned her that nobody would want a doctor serving their beer.

She was tired, anyway. And she did not want Matthew to like and accept her now because he knew she was in such a sterling profession.

If only he could have believed the best about her all by himself.

Sandra said he was angry. And she didn't care if it was true or not. She already knew that she had to go. She had run out of choices. She loved him desperately. Maybe pathetically.

Maybe pathetically enough to use the child that grew within her to try and hold him.

She pressed her stomach with affection for her unborn child. Maybe something pretty wonderful had come out of her shattered dreams for one perfect, shining summer after all. She crept into the bedroom and retrieved her already packed suitcase from under her bed.

She walked one last time down the rickety boardwalk in front of the cabins, and stood for a long time looking down at the sleeping lodge, the moody lake beyond it. The stars winked over her, as if they were trying to tell her something. "Sometimes you only get one invitation to this particular dance, Charity. Take it..." Her throat closed.

She couldn't. What could she do, anyway? Just tell him. Matthew, I love you and what are you going to do about it?

What if he said nothing? What if he said he was going to marry Sandra after all? What if he, like every other man in her life, could not accept her professional standing?

She needed to get away from here. She had to think. She had to get away from this magical place, and away from his close proximity, to think clearly.

She knocked on Nelson's cabin door.

He came to the door, shirtless, in a pair of old sweatpants.

"What's up, Doc?" he quipped, and then laughed with thorough enjoyment of his own humor.

"I need a ride, Nelson. I need a ride into town."

He looked as if he was going to protest, but his eyes caught her face, and for the first time since she had known him Nelson was one hundred percent a grown-up.

His eyes softened with compassion. "You got it," he said quietly. "No questions asked."

CHAPTER TEN

MATTHEW BLAKE felt alive. It was as if he could feel the life force vibrating through his being, and tingling out of his fingertips.

His energy was incredible. He felt like singing.

Did near-death experiences do this to everyone?

He smiled. He knew that what he was feeling didn't have much to do with his brush with death.

It had something to do with opening his eyes and looking into her eyes. And seeing. And knowing.

Charity Marlowe loved him.

Dr. Charity Marlowe.

He opened the door to his hospital room, keeping one hand tightly clenched on the back of this *thing* they had given him to wear.

"Nurse!" he bellowed.

She came scurrying, a good roar doing what his call light had not.

"Mr. Blake, you get back into bed this minute."

The young woman was all of twenty. Where had she learned to address full-grown men in that schoolmarmish tone of voice?

He glowered at her. "Mr. Blake is leaving. Where are my clothes?"

"The doctor is just making his rounds now. If you'll just be patient . . ."

"Patience," he growled, "is not my strong suit. I am not a patient patient. Where are my clothes?"

"You are not leaving!"

Amusement bubbled up in him at this tiny little thing with her hands planted firmly on her hips presuming to tell him what he was going to do.

He decided against letting her know he found her amusing. Instead he narrowed his eyes at her.

"I have an appointment with my own personal physician, and I don't want to be late. Get my clothes, *now.*" He slammed the door on her indignant face. His clothes were delivered, a haughty sniff the woman's only protest.

A young doctor came through the door. "I hear you're leaving us," he said with an easygoing grin. "Let me have a look at you before you go. How are you feeling?"

"Never better," Matthew said, eyeing the young man thoughtfully. "Tell me, what was it like going to medical school?"

The doctor looked surprised. "A grind. Thinking of changing careers?"

"No. I just wondered if someone who had spent a few years in medical school might take a job away from the field...just for a summer. Maybe at a resort or something."

"I sure would have, if I'd had the chance. You're pretty burned-out after interning. You seem fit as a fiddle, Mr. Blake. Close call, though. Watch those almonds, eh?" And he disappeared out of the door, his white jacket flapping around him.

Matthew rented a car. He could have called and had someone come to get him, but it would have taken longer, and he wanted to see her now. Ten minutes ago. Why hadn't she come to the hospital?

Because Sandra had. He remembered opening his eyes, and seeing it was Sandra holding his hand, and feeling shocked. He had thought it was Charity.

Sandra, he thought wearily, as he began the curving drive down the east side of the lake. Sandra.

At first he had been simply bowled over by her enormous beauty, her laughter, her charm. They had a whirlwind romance, and after a few months she'd started hinting for a ring.

And he had thought, well, why not? He'd never met a woman who made him feel that way, and, let's face it, he wasn't getting any younger.

But it was after he'd given her the ring that the cracks had begun to appear in her facade. It was as if she had been playing a part with all her might for several months, but it had sapped her energy. She couldn't keep it up.

With growing awareness—and wariness—he had started to notice that Sandra worked at being what he wanted her to be, or at least what she presumed he wanted her to be. He'd felt like a specimen being studied. What made him laugh? What foods did he like? What kind of clothes did he wear? What activities did he do?

He began to feel uncomfortable with being someone else's total reason for getting out of bed in the morning.

He began to realize he didn't *know* Sandra. He'd been so flattered by her unflagging attention, her unflagging efforts to please him, that he didn't have a clue who she was. And he wasn't very happy with what that said about him.

He tried to find out. What do *you* like? What do *you* do? But she claimed she liked being with him, she liked making him happy, and she liked doing what he did.

He was beginning to feel a little trapped by Miss Bamfield's attention.

And she was so hooked into him that she sensed that changing of mood almost immediately, and the facade split open a little wider.

She became extraordinarily jealous. She whined that he didn't love her. She pushed for a wedding date.

He drew further away, and she pushed closer in. She began showing up at whatever hotel he was working at during the day, claiming to have been just passing. She grilled him about women she saw in hotel lobbies, as if he knew each one personally. She began to shower him with desperate gifts.

He broke the engagement, stunned by how easily he'd been duped by her. Stunned that he hadn't known from the first moment that something was wrong with her.

It was after he broke the engagement that the real craziness started. She phoned him at all hours of the day and night, ranting sometimes, crying others. She sat in front of his house in her car. She sent him letters and gifts.

He pitied her, and he didn't know how to handle it. It was now painfully obvious to him that he was dealing with a very fragile mental state, and he didn't want to be responsible for setting it off balance irreparably.

The problems at Anpetuwi probably hadn't warranted his taking a trip to Canada, but several thousand miles of rough, cold ocean between him and Sandra Bamfield had been too tempting to resist.

His own mental health was suffering. He felt somehow responsible for the way she was behaving, as if he should have spotted it sooner, caught on sooner. He'd always been a superb judge of character, but now he doubted himself.

Enter Charity Marlowe. The attraction he had felt to her had been instant. But look where that had got him last time. And he no longer took things at face value. How could he? He was *looking* for signs that people were not as they first appeared to be, and Charity seemed to be a case of history repeating itself.

First, he saw her looking at him through binoculars, something he wouldn't have put past a man-hungry shark like Sandra. And secondly, he was very aware that she was no waitress. Any more than Sandra had been a wholesome, beautiful, normal girl looking to settle down.

So, he gave himself a red light on the beautiful Miss Marlowe, only to find he couldn't make himself obey it. She intrigued him and enticed him and infuriated him.

He was beginning to feel as if he had just switched roller coasters—from one set of emotional turmoil to another. And then, as if he weren't confused enough, Sandra arrived in person.

He couldn't believe it. His temper, held so carefully in check around Sandra's fragile emotions, exploded. Unfortunately, she reacted to his temper in just the manner he had feared she might. She fell completely apart. She wept until she threw up. She pulled out chunks of her hair. Finally, she told him if he sent her home she'd commit suicide.

He let her stay, thinking it was the "kind" thing to do. Thinking that if he ignored her, didn't show even a whisper of interest in her, she would give up and go home under her own steam, thereby allowing her to rescue some of her dignity. And one thing he did know about the *real* Sandra was that she had a very low tolerance for boredom, and that she got bored very easily. He thought she might not last a week at Anpetuwi.

So there he was, caught in a trap of his own making—being nice to a woman he didn't like, and mean to one he did, and as mixed up as a schoolboy in short pants.

Having Sandra there did increase his awareness that a person could look fabulous and still be harboring a darkness inside them, and it increased his suspicion of Charity.

How could anybody be as wonderful as she appeared to be? No one could be all those things—intelligent, kind, compassionate, sexy. Who was she really? And what did she really want from him, and Anpetuwi?

Then his grandmother's jewels disappeared, and he had the oddest sensation of *wanting* Charity to have done it. Because if she hadn't done it, if she was exactly as she appeared to be—warm, vibrant, witty, and sensual—he was going to have to marry her, and he knew it. He was going to have to admit he loved her and couldn't live without her, and that was a hard thing for a man who had always been one hundred percent in control, and who had always been one hundred percent independent, and one hundred percent rational, to do.

But, standing in her bathroom, with her looking at him with those lovely blue eyes, her whole soul looking him in the face, her integrity undeniable, he knew the truth. He loved her. And believed in her.

And he got out of there fast, before she could see it, some masculine fear in him that if she knew how he felt she would use his vulnerability against him.

And it was as he turned from her, that jewel box in his hand, that he suddenly knew who had taken those jewels, and his anger carried him away from Charity's pain and her need.

He knew, though, that he had to let that anger die a bit before he confronted Sandra. He didn't feel she could emotionally handle his anger. And he knew he had to get rid of her.

Then, sitting through a very strained dinner, preoccupied, and miserable, he let his guard down, and ate that bloody cake loaded with finely crushed almonds...

He remembered Charity saying something about Anpetuwi being a bit magic—it could turn even bad things around so that they were good.

And last night, when he had ingested an almond—the absolutely worst thing that could happen to him—something good had happened.

Good? Wondrous. Sublime. He had seen that Charity loved him. He had seen who she really was. He had seen that Charity Marlowe was exactly what she appeared to be. *Exactly.* An extremely bright young woman who cared about other people to the depths of her soul. Who cared about *him* to the depths of her soul, even though he was, in his own mind, completely undeserving of her love.

In that moment, he had known he could trust her—with his very life, as it were. She would not use his love of her to hurt him.

And he had also seen, with a flash of insight, that being "kind" to Sandra was the worst cruelty he could inflict on her. It gave the poor girl hope, where there was none. It led her to believe that her deluded behavior was within the realm of the acceptable when it was not.

Last night, he had reached beyond his exhaustion into some reserve of strength and told Sandra how things were. He had told her, so that today he could be free—free to go to Charity and tell her about this astonishing feeling inside of him.

He had told Sandra to go and get her things from the lodge and go. He had told her she needed professional help, and he hoped she would find it. He had told her that if she continued to harass him he would call the police.

They were hard words and he had trouble saying them. He had trouble, when she began to cry, her face that of a heartbroken child's, not to reach out and hold her one last time. He didn't hate her, and he certainly didn't want to hurt her, but he knew he had just done the best thing he could ever do for Sandra Bamfield.

He pulled the car into the parking lot, and got out. He paused and looked over Anpetuwi, the verdant green of the trees, the azure of the sky, the moody blue of the lake, beyond.

Anpetuwi, which had given his family the gift of love, generation after generation. Anpetuwi, where he had come with his hurt and confusion, and Anpetuwi, which had not disappointed him, taking him and holding him in its gentle heart as a mother held a child.

She felt it, too. Charity felt the same mystery in this place that he felt, that his mother had felt before him.

It was as if all creation conspired here to show people the mystery and the marvel of love.

He walked, his pace swift, down the twisting path, then hesitated where it veered off to the staff cabins. Would she be there or on the beach? Should he sweep her into his arms and kiss the daylights out of her first, or should he slow down for explanations?

He broke into a trot as he headed up the path to the staff cabins.

He pounded on their door, and Mandy came to it, her head in a towel. He laughed out loud.

"You Marlowe girls and your towels."

A warning light blinked dimly inside his brain when Mandy didn't respond with her usual good humor.

"Make that Marlowe girl, singular," she told him. She was looking at him with recrimination.

"What?"

"Charity's gone."

"She's gone? Where?"

"She didn't tell me. She only left me a little note. She said she couldn't tell me because you would probably get it out of me, snake that you are."

"She called me a snake?" he asked hollowly.

"No. I did. She wouldn't appreciate me telling you this, but she loved you. She believed the best of you."

"I know."

"You know? And you still treated her like that?"

"I didn't always know. And I didn't always know what I was feeling either. But I do now. Where do you think she'd go?"

Mandy was watching him warily, and then suddenly her face relaxed. "You love her, don't you, Matthew?"

"Yes. I'm going to ask her to marry me."

"Really?" Mandy squealed. She flung herself into Matthew's arms. "I knew it was you! I knew from the first moment you were the man for her."

"Now how did you know that?" Matthew asked with amusement.

"I'm a witch with magic binoculars," Mandy said, wrinkling her nose at him. "You know, Charity doesn't do things like that."

"Well, she was doing it the first time I laid eyes on her!"

"She occasionally can be talked into doing something a little silly, but not often." Mandy hesitated and took a deep breath. "Matthew, Charity would never falsify an application form."

"I know that," he said softly. "I've known that for some time. My heart told me she wouldn't. My mind told she couldn't. But there was the application sitting in my file trying to make a liar out of me."

"I did it."

He had never seen Mandy look contrite before, and he decided, wickedly, to make her suffer a bit before he let her off the hook. He let the silence drag, long and hard, and then he finally spoke.

"Mandy, I suppose if you and I are going to be related there's no hope at all I'm ever going to be able to tamp down that irrepressible side of yours, is there?"

"No hope at all," Mandy agreed happily, beaming at him. "And I want my binos back."

"Binos?"

"Binoculars."

He laughed. "I'm glad I can't change you," he said with real affection. "I'll trade you your 'binos' for information that might lead me to the whereabouts of Dr. Charity Marlowe."

"Deal."

CHARITY WAS exhausted. Thank goodness Timmy, who had hurt his knee at hockey practice, was her last patient scheduled at the walk-in clinic today.

Unfortunately, the ten-year-old was looking at her mutinously. "I'm not taking off my pants in front of a *girl.*"

"Fine," she said crisply, snapping closed his file. "Dr. Clark will be back in a week. By then, if there's something wrong with your knee, the damage should be permanent. But what's a career in the National Hockey League, anyway?"

The jeans came off and she examined the knee without any further problem. Five minutes later the midget ex-chauvinist was on his way.

Charity had a look at herself in the mirror and sighed. She wasn't quite sure how Timmy had figured out she was a girl. The streaking was out of her hair, and she'd cut it shorter. She'd reverted to her glasses because she thought they made her look older and more respectable, somehow, the way people wanted a doctor to look. In two weeks, her light summer tan was already fading.

Her one shining summer was over.

The office nurse came in, and clucked sympathetically. "I hate to even ask, but Dr. Marlowe, can you see one more? He says he's really sick and feverish. A healthier-looking man I've never seen, but—"

Charity held out her hand for the file, and flipped it open. Matthew Blake. "No!" she cried after the nurse.

"Too late." He was already standing in the doorway, looking at her, and looking damned pleased with himself, too.

He was in a beautifully cut suit that molded that fine physique and made her blush with wanting.

"You're not sick," she said accusingly.

"I am too." He shrugged off his suit jacket.

"What are you doing?" she gasped.

He undid his buttons, and peeled off his shirt. She stared, aghast, at the fine-honed beauty of that chest. She closed her eyes against it.

"Put your shirt back on this minute," she ordered through clenched teeth.

"But I have to show you where it hurts."

"Your head is going to hurt where I hit you with this clipboard. Now put your shirt on, and get out of here."

"Uh-uh."

His hand closed, warm and strong around hers. Her eyes flew open.

"This is where it hurts."

He guided her hand to the hard surface of his chest and placed it above his heart. He let go of her hand, but it remained there, captured by the silk texture of his skin, by the warmth that radiated from him.

"It hurts here?" she gulped.

"My heart hurts," he said softly.

"But you told the nurse you were feverish," she said stupidly. She still didn't move her hand.

"I am. Feverish with longing."

She snatched her hand back, turned away from him, and focused furiously on her clipboard.

But he was behind her now, his hand heavy on the nape of her neck.

"You look beautiful, Charity."

"Now I'm starting to believe you really are sick," she said with a snort.

He spun her around, and she found herself locked in that steady blue gaze.

"I always knew there was something not quite you about that getup you wore at the lodge."

"You seemed to think I was very sexy," she reminded him sharply.

He laughed. "You don't really think that has a thing to do with what you wear or what you have on your face, do you?"

"As a matter of fact—"

He touched her short hair tenderly, reached up, and slowly slid the glasses from her nose. "Every man dreams of this—"

"Give me back those glasses."

"Of being the one who finds the diamond in a lump of coal, who finds the fire at the center of the earth."

His lips were descending on her. She slapped a hand over his lips in pure self-defense. He kissed her hand.

"Matthew, what do you want from me?"

"You saved my life."

"So say thank you, and leave."

"I prefer the Oriental tradition."

"Which is?" she asked nervously. His tongue tickled her hand.

"To give your life to the one who saved it."

"Oh, really!" She wished he'd quit doing that to her hand—but she didn't want to move it in case he moved on to her lips.

"My life belongs to you, now, Dr. Marlowe. What are you going to do about that?"

She remembered thinking, once, in a desperate moment, that she should just go to Matthew and say, I love you. What are you going to do about that? She was not prepared for a very similar question being thrown at her.

"What would you like me to do about it?" she countered. She could stand it no more. She jerked her hand away from him, and shoved it in her pocket.

The devil had the audacity to grin at her, as if he knew precisely the fires he had lit inside the center of the earth.

"Well," he said slowly, "you could put your arms around my neck, press your soft body into me and let me know you accept my offering."

"I don't know what you're offering. It sounds like sex. Big deal."

"It always seemed like a pretty big deal to me," he said. "I could have sworn it seemed like a pretty big deal to you, too."

"It's not enough!" she cried. As soon as the words were out of her mouth she regretted them.

"Hmm." His voice was noncommittal, and his eyes narrow. "What's enough?"

She was proudly and stubbornly silent.

"Would it be enough if you had someone to hold during the long, cold nights?" A strange tenderness had entered his voice, and roughened it. "Would it be enough if you had someone to laugh with? To share your most secret self with? To play with? To have babies with? Would that be enough?"

She ducked her head, and began to cry.

He touched her chin, and forced her eyes to his. And then she saw what she had not seen before. The gentleness in those deep eyes. The welcome. The yearning to be with her.

"Would it be enough," he continued, his voice husky with emotion, "if I stood beside you, before the whole world, and took your hand in mine and promised you I would be there, in sickness and in health? For better or worse? In good times and in tough times? Would that be enough?"

The sobs were shaking her, the tears making his handsome face wobble in front of her vision.

"Would it be enough," he whispered, "if I told you I will love you for all time, that my heart has found its resting place, and my soul has found its mate? Would that be enough?"

"M-M-Matthew, p-please stop."

"I can't. I can't stop until you accept the gift I lay before you. Will you, Charity? Will you accept the gift of my life? Will you give me the gift of yours in return?"

"I'm pregnant," she wailed.

His eyes widened in surprise, and then she found herself pulled hard into the wall of his chest, his arms wrapped tight around her. She felt safe and warm and as if she had come home.

"Oh, Charity," he said, his voice exquisitely gentle and filled with wonder. "Why didn't you tell me?"

"I thought you'd feel trapped," she whispered. "I didn't want you to feel trapped."

"And so you felt trapped instead," he guessed. "You must have felt alone. Afraid. With no one to share the most special moments of your life with. Woman, I do believe you love me. But absolutely no more misguided nobility. We're in this together."

"You're happy," she said softly, tilting back her head so that she could look into his face.

"There are two little mischief makers at Anpetuwi," he said.

"Nelson and Mandy?"

"No. The god of love and the god of fertility. They haven't been wrong yet."

She sagged against him. "I have been afraid," she confided. "Not sure what tomorrow would hold. Not sure what this would do to my career." She hesitated. "Not sure that I would ever again be able to love someone the way I love you."

"When you choose love, Charity, you can have everything you want. A career, and a family. Love doesn't take anything away. It makes everything possible, and it makes everything shine."

And it was true. She looked back over that stormy summer and was surprised to see each scene, even the ones that had seemed rather painful at the time, shining with an almost holy silver light.

He took her lips with passion.

"Matthew," she gasped, surfacing a long time later. "We can't. Not here. The nurse—"

"Sent her home," he muttered thickly. "And she listened to me. There was no mistaking that I was a very sick man."

"I know just the thing," the doctor told him.

INDULGE A LITTLE 6947 SWEEPSTAKES
NO PURCHASE NECESSARY

HERE'S HOW THE SWEEPSTAKES WORKS:
The Harlequin Reader Service shipments for January, February and March 1994 will contain, respectively, coupons for entry into three prize drawings: a trip for two to San Francisco, an Alaskan cruise for two and a trip for two to Hawaii. To be eligible for any drawing using an Entry Coupon, simply complete and mail according to directions.

There is no obligation to continue as a Reader Service subscriber to enter and be eligible for any prize drawing. You may also enter any drawing by hand printing your name and address on a 3" x 5" card and the destination of the prize you wish that entry to be considered for (i.e., San Francisco trip, Alaskan cruise or Hawaiian trip). Send your 3" x 5" entries to: Indulge a Little 6947 Sweepstakes, c/o Prize Destination you wish that entry to be considered for, P.O. Box 1315, Buffalo, NY 14269-1315, U.S.A. or Indulge a Little 6947 Sweepstakes, P.O. Box 610, Fort Erie, Ontario L2A 5X3, Canada.

To be eligible for the San Francisco trip, entries must be received by 4/30/94; for the Alaskan cruise, 5/31/94; and the Hawaiian trip, 6/30/94. No responsibility is assumed for lost, late or misdirected mail. Sweepstakes open to residents of the U.S. (except Puerto Rico) and Canada, 18 years of age or older. All applicable laws and regulations apply. Sweepstakes void wherever prohibited.

For a copy of the Official Rules, send a self-addressed, stamped envelope (WA residents need not affix return postage) to: Indulge a Little 6947 Rules, P.O. Box 4631, Blair, NE 68009, U.S.A.

INDR93

INDULGE A LITTLE 6947 SWEEPSTAKES
NO PURCHASE NECESSARY

HERE'S HOW THE SWEEPSTAKES WORKS:
The Harlequin Reader Service shipments for January, February and March 1994 will contain, respectively, coupons for entry into three prize drawings: a trip for two to San Francisco, an Alaskan cruise for two and a trip for two to Hawaii. To be eligible for any drawing using an Entry Coupon, simply complete and mail according to directions.

There is no obligation to continue as a Reader Service subscriber to enter and be eligible for any prize drawing. You may also enter any drawing by hand printing your name and address on a 3" x 5" card and the destination of the prize you wish that entry to be considered for (i.e., San Francisco trip, Alaskan cruise or Hawaiian trip). Send your 3" x 5" entries to: Indulge a Little 6947 Sweepstakes, c/o Prize Destination you wish that entry to be considered for, P.O. Box 1315, Buffalo, NY 14269-1315, U.S.A. or Indulge a Little 6947 Sweepstakes, P.O. Box 610, Fort Erie, Ontario L2A 5X3, Canada.

To be eligible for the San Francisco trip, entries must be received by 4/30/94; for the Alaskan cruise, 5/31/94; and the Hawaiian trip, 6/30/94. No responsibility is assumed for lost, late or misdirected mail. Sweepstakes open to residents of the U.S. (except Puerto Rico) and Canada, 18 years of age or older. All applicable laws and regulations apply. Sweepstakes void wherever prohibited.

For a copy of the Official Rules, send a self-addressed, stamped envelope (WA residents need not affix return postage) to: Indulge a Little 6947 Rules, P.O. Box 4631, Blair, NE 68009, U.S.A.

INDR93

INDULGE A LITTLE
SWEEPSTAKES

OFFICIAL ENTRY COUPON

This entry must be received by: APRIL 30, 1994
This month's winner will be notified by: MAY 15, 1994
Trip must be taken between: JUNE 30, 1994-JUNE 30, 1995

YES, I want to win the San Francisco vacation for two. I understand that the prize includes round-trip airfare, first-class hotel, rental car and pocket money as revealed on the "wallet" scratch-off card.

Name____

Address __________________________ Apt. __________________

City____

State/Prov.____________________ Zip/Postal Code_______________

Daytime phone number________________________________
(Area Code)

Account #_______________________________________

Return entries with invoice in envelope provided. Each book in this shipment has two entry coupons—and the more coupons you enter, the better your chances of winning!

 MONTH1

INDULGE A LITTLE
SWEEPSTAKES

OFFICIAL ENTRY COUPON

This entry must be received by: APRIL 30, 1994
This month's winner will be notified by: MAY 15, 1994
Trip must be taken between: JUNE 30, 1994-JUNE 30, 1995

YES, I want to win the San Francisco vacation for two. I understand that the prize includes round-trip airfare, first-class hotel, rental car and pocket money as revealed on the "wallet" scratch-off card.

Name____

Address __________________________ Apt. __________________

City____

State/Prov.____________________ Zip/Postal Code_______________

Daytime phone number________________________________
(Area Code)

Account #_______________________________________

Return entries with invoice in envelope provided. Each book in this shipment has two entry coupons—and the more coupons you enter, the better your chances of winning!

© 1993 HARLEQUIN ENTERPRISES LTD. MONTH1